LOVE IN THE MOON
Barbara Cartland

D1823813

NEW ENGLISH LIBRARY/TIMES MIRROR

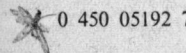 0 450 05192 7

ABOUT THE AUTHOR

Barbara Cartland, the world's most famous romantic novelist, who is also an historian, playwright, lecturer, political speaker and television personality, has now written nearly 300 books and sold over 200 million books over the world.

She has also had many historical works published and has written four autobiographies as well as the biographies of her mother and that of her brother, Ronald Cartland, who was the first Member of Parliament to be killed in the last war. This book has a preface by Sir Winston Churchill.

She has recently completed a novel, 'Love at the Helm', with the help and inspiration of the late Admiral of the Fleet, the Earl Mountbatten of Burma. This is being sold for the Mountbatten Memorial Trust.

Miss Cartland in 1978 sang an Album of Love Songs with the Royal Philharmonic Orchestra.

In 1976 by writing twenty-one books, she broke the world record and has continued for the following three years with 24, 20, and 23.

In private life Barbara Cartland, who is a Dame of the Order of St. John of Jerusalem, Chairman of the St. John Council in Hertfordshire and Deputy President of the St. John Ambulance Brigade, has fought for better conditions and salaries for Midwives and Nurses.

She has championed the cause for old people, had the law altered regarding gypsies and founded the first Romany Gypsy camp in the world.

Barbara Cartland is deeply interested in Vitamin Therapy and is President of the British National Association for Health.

OTHER BOOKS BY BARBARA CARTLAND
– total over 280 books.

Romantic Novels
over 250, the most recently published being:

From Hell to Heaven
Pride and the Poor Princess
The Lioness and the Lily
The Kiss of Life
Afraid
The Horizons of Love
Love in the Moon
The Waltz of Hearts
Dollars for the Duke
Dreams Do Come True
A Night of Gaiety
Count the Stars
Winged Magic
A Portrait of Love
Gift of the Gods
The Heart of the Clan
An Innocent in Russia
A Shaft of Sunlight
Love Wins

The Dream and the Glory (in aid of the St. John Ambulance Brigade)

Autobiographical and Biographical

The Isthmus Years 1919-1939
The Years of Opportunity 1939-1945
I Search for Rainbows 1945-1976
We Danced All Night 1919-1929
Ronald Cartland (with a Foreword by Sir Winston Churchill)
Polly My Wonderful Mother
I Seek the Miraculous

Historical:

Bewitching Women
The Outrageous Queen (The Story of Queen Christina of Sweden)
The Scandalous Life of King Carol
The Private Life of King Charles II
The Private Life of Elizabeth, Empress of Austria
Josephine, Empress of France
Diane de Poitiers
Metternich – The Passionate Diplomat

Sociology:

You in the Home

The Fascinating Forties
Marriage for Moderns
Be Vivid, Be Vital
Love, Life and Sex
Vitamins for Vitality
Husbands and Wives
Etiquette
The Many Facets of Love
Sex and the Teenager
The Book of Charm
Living Together
The Youth Secret
The Magic of Honey
Barbara Cartland's Book of Beauty and Health
Men are Wonderful

Cookery:

Barbara Cartland's Health Food Cookery Book
Food for Love
Magic of Honey Cookbook
Recipes for Lovers

Editor of:

The Common Problems by Ronald Cartland (with a preface by
the Rt. Hon. the Earl of Selborne, P.C.)

Barbara Cartland's Library of Love

Barbara Cartland's Library of Ancient Wisdom

Drama:

Blood Money
French Dressing

Philosophy

Touch the Stars

Radio Operetta:

The Rose and the Violet (Music by Mark Lubbock) performed in
1942

Radio Plays:

The Caged Bird: an episode in the Life of Elizabeth Empress of
Austria.
Performed in 1957

General:

Barbara Cartland's Book of Useless Information, with a Foreword by The Earl Mountbatten of Burma
(In Aid of the United World Colleges)

Love and Lovers (Picture Book)

The Light of Love (Prayer Book)

Barbara Cartland's Scrapbook, in Aid of the Royal Photographic Museum

Verse:

Lines on Life and Love

Music:

An Album of Love Songs sung with the Royal Philharmonic Orchestra

Magazine:

Barbara Cartland's World of Romance (published in the U.S.A.)

Special Publication:

Love at the Helm
Inspired and helped by Admiral of the Fleet Earl Mountbatten of Burma, in Aid of the Mountbatten Memorial Trust.

AUTHOR'S NOTE

When I visited the Dordogne area this year (1980) I thought it beautiful and I also enjoyed passing through the prolific and famous vineyards round Bordeaux. The depression as I related in this story, started in the early 1860's when phylloxera was introduced to France by infected stock from America.

By the time the nature of the disease was fully understood the pest had spread so rapidly that little could be done to check it.

In Périgord the worst ravages occurred in the late 1870's and by 1892 the area devoted to vines was only a fifth of what it had been twenty years earlier.

But though the population is still less than it should be, now crops are well established. Strawberries are sent daily during the season by lorry to Paris; Dordogne is the leading *department* in France for the production of walnuts; tobacco is often to the peasant farmers their best source of cash.

A dozen papermills employ 1,500 workers, trees, fruit and pedigree bulls employ many others.

But tourism beats them all and the fascination of 'a corner of the moon' lies in the battle cry of a Périgordin made a thousand years ago.

"A stone for the wicked, a loving heart for one's friends, a sword for the enemy – if you can find all three, you are a Périgordin."

CHAPTER ONE
1878

The Earl of Langstone helped himself to another lamb cutlet from a large silver dish as the door of the Dining-Room opened and his sister came in.

She was dressed in a riding-habit and he looked up from the breakfast table with a smile to say:

"You are late, and I suppose the excuse is the usual one, that your horse kept you."

"Of course he did!" Lady Canéda Lang replied. "Who else would be so alluring at this hour of the morning?"

Her brother laughed.

"That is for you to say. What happened with Warrington last night?"

Canéda did not reply as she helped herself from a side table, to bacon and eggs. Then as she sat down opposite her brother, she said:

"I think, Harry, you will have to speak to him. He is becoming a nuisance. He made me go with him into the Conservatory, and kept me there practically by force!"

"It would save a lot of trouble if you would accept him," the Earl replied.

His sister made a derisive sound.

"I have no intention of marrying Lord Warrington, or any other of those half-wits who have proposed to me these last two months. I keep remembering they would not be so keen if you had not come into a title and a very large fortune."

The Earl laughed.

"A cynic at nineteen!" he teased. "My dear Canéda, you are a very pretty girl, and it is not surprising that men throw their hearts at your feet, especially when you are well gowned."

Canéda's eyes softened.

"That I owe to you, Harry, and there is not a moment of the day when I do not enjoy feeling like a Princess in a fairy tale and remember that my wardrobe is full of other gowns just as delectable."

"I have the idea," her brother answered, "that you are fishing for compliments, but I am sure you know without my telling you that fine feathers make fine birds."

"That is true," Canéda replied, "but, Harry, it is exciting, is it not, to be rich, to be living here, having all those wonderful, wonderful horses you have bought me to ride, as well as Ariel?"

"What have you been teaching him this morning?" the Earl enquired.

"I have two new tricks for you to see as soon as you have the time. You never believe me, but I swear he understands every word I say to him! However many gorgeous horses fill your stable, there will never be one as marvellous as Ariel!"

The Earl did not argue.

He knew what his sister felt about the horse she had had since it was a foal, and which when they were poor she had looked after herself.

It had been an extravagance for her to have a horse of her own in addition to those shared between father and son.

Canéda had always been crazy about horses ever since she was a child and Ariel, the Earl had to admit, was as a result of her teaching, a very remarkable horse indeed.

But it was almost with the same enthusiasm as his sister showed, and with a sense of great satisfaction, that he thought of the stables at Langstone Park which were now filled to capacity.

He had plans being drawn up for extending the buildings to accommodate more horses which he had every intention of buying in the near future.

It was only nine months ago that Harry Lang had woken

up one morning to find incredibly and with a distinct sense of shock that he had become an Earl.

There had been three lives between him, the only son of a younger son, to the title and estates of the Earls of Langstone. His father had been killed in a hunting accident two years previously and now a storm in the Irish Sea had caused the death of his uncle and his two sons, who were returning to England from the Emerald Isle.

Because Harry's father had never got on with his elder brother and it was up to the head of the family to finance the other members of it, they had been extremely poor.

But they had also, Canéda often thought, been much happier in their small Manor House in an equally small village than their relations who lived in grandeur in the family mansion and had apparently a huge fortune to play with.

The Earl's two sons, both of whom were older than Harry, enjoyed themselves so much amongst the gaieties and frivolities of London that they had both, despite insistent pressure from their parents and other relations, refused to marry.

One pursued social beauties who were inevitably already married; the other preferred the exceedingly attractive actresses who were to be found on stage at Drury Lane or the Gaiety Theatre, which was already becoming famous for its lovely women.

In consequence, they were both nearly thirty and unmarried, so that Harry at twenty-four stepped into their inheritance and became the 9th Earl.

To Canéda it was as if fate had waved a magic wand over them, so that while sitting like Cinderella among the ashes she was suddenly transplanted in a 'pumpkin' carriage to a Prince's Palace.

Langstone Park, which she had visited only a few times in her life, certainly justified that description.

Enormous, in the grandiose style of Blenheim Palace and Castle Howard and built by the same architect,

Vanbrugh, it looked breath-taking as they drove down the drive.

Although Harry said very little, she had known by the pulse throbbing at the side of his cheek that he was as thrilled as she was.

There had, first of all, been the funeral of the late Earl and his two sons, when the great house had been filled with relatives from all over England, who had flocked there not only to pay their respects to the dead, but also to inspect critically and a little apprehensively his inheritance.

Because Gerald Lang had paid little attention to his relatives and they to him in the past twenty five years, it was obvious they were all wondering what the new head of the family would be like, and if Harry would live up to its traditions.

It would have been impossible, Canéda had thought, watching their sideways glances at her brother, for them not to be impressed by his appearance.

He was tall, broad-shouldered, fair and handsome in the Lang tradition.

In fact it was difficult to imagine that he was not entirely English since his mother had been French.

Canéda on the other hand, resembled the exquisite Clémentine de Bantôme whom Gerald Lang had seen when he was exploring France, and had instantly determined she should be his wife.

It was not only the Langs who thought it an undoubted mistake for one of their family to marry a foreigner, but also the Bantômes, who were furious that an impecunious and to them unimportant Englishman should persuade Clémentine to run away with him on the eve of her marriage to another man.

The *Comtes* de Bantôme had always given themselves great airs.

Their estate in the Périgord region of France on the banks of the Dordogne had been theirs for centuries and they were also rich and powerful.

Therefore like all French aristocrats they were determined that the noble strain in their blood should be matched by the nobility of those who sought their children's hand in marriage.

Clémentine had been betrothed to the *Duc* de Saumac, a man very much older than she was.

In running away with her, Gerald Lang had offended not only the de Bantômes, but the *Duc* who was equally as powerful in the Loire Valley where his estate was situated.

It was an insult that was translated into a vendetta against Gerald Lang which had its repercussions in various ways.

The first thing Gerald found after he married Clémentine, was that it was impossible for him to visit France without being arrested on some trumped up charge or another.

At first he could hardly believe that it was not just chance that he, an ordinary tourist, was being continually taken to the nearest *gendarmarie* for questioning.

He soon discovered who was behind it and it became such a persecution that he knew it was impossible for either himself or his wife ever to stay in Paris again.

He also suffered insults and hostility in London, where the French Ambassador had obviously had instructions from the *Duc* to stir up trouble.

It was therefore fortunate that Gerald Lang had no wish to shine socially, and was perfectly content to settle down in the country with his wife, his children and, when he could afford them, his horses.

Fortunately, as he was such an outstanding rider, he more often rode other people's horses than his own.

Neighbouring Squires liked the Langs and often lent both father and son their horses to ride in races, steeplechases, point-to-points and out hunting.

Because she was so attractive they would also gladly have mounted Canéda, but she had been content for the last three years with her own horse which she loved more than anything else in the whole world.

For Harry to become the owner of what was even before he added to it a first-class stable and know that he would have every facility for racing his own horses, was a joy beyond words.

The brother and sister had become an instant success when they opened Langstone House in Grosvenor Square.

They had paid a perfunctory gesture in respect of mourning their uncle, and had appeared in London in the sixth month to take the Social World by storm.

Harry's looks and charm in addition to his title and wealth threw every door open to him, and Canéda had a very different type of success, but one that was no less gratifying.

If Harry looked like his English forebears, Canéda was like her mother.

She was small, her dark hair had mysterious blue lights in it, and her oval face was dominated by two huge eyes outlined by long dark eye-lashes.

But there the French resemblance ended and Canéda's eyes were the same blue as her brother's, making her already lovely face even more arresting because the combination was so unusual.

She was beautiful enough to make any man who looked at her want to look again, and once his eyes were caught by her blue ones he became her captive, and there was no escape.

"It cannot be true, Harry!" Canéda said breathlessly a few weeks after they had been in London. "I have had no less than three proposals of marriage tonight!"

"I am not surprised," Harry replied.

He had been aware during the Ball which they had both attended that his sister shone like a star amongst the other rather gauche, tongue-tied and shy young women of the same age.

Even compared with the dazzling, sophisticated older women she seemed to have a quality that was missing in them and which, even though she was his sister, Harry thought had something irresistible about it.

It was perhaps her vivacity, the way her eyes shone and her lips curved in a smile, that made her appear more alive than anybody he had ever met.

Because brother and sister were so close to each other and because they had all through their childhood had a companionship that was unusually intimate, Harry felt very protective about Canéda and was determined that no-one should rush her into marriage.

Elderly aunts who had constituted themselves Canéda's chaperons, were already pressing him to make her accept one of the very advantageous offers she had received.

"Lord Warrington is exceedingly rich," they said, "and his house in Huntingdonshire is almost as fine as Langstone Park."

Harry had not been responsive, and they had gone on almost angrily:

"We are told that Canéda rejected the Earl of Headingly without even listening to what he had to say! How can she be so foolish?"

Harry who had his own opinion about the Earl of Headingly, had not been very impressed.

"Canéda can marry who and when she wants," he said, "and the longer she takes about it the better I shall be pleased, as I like her with me."

"You have no right to spoil her chances," his aunts protested, but Harry had only laughed.

He knew what his sister felt about marriage, and he could understand how the men who pursued her must feel frustrated at her refusal to take them seriously.

He was also aware that Lord Warrington in particular was growing more and more desperate.

But before he could say any more, the Butler came into the room carrying the morning's post on a silver salver.

There were three letters on it which he offered to Harry saying:

"Mr. Barnet's compliments, M'Lord, and as he thought these would be private communications he didn't open them."

"Thank you, Dawson."

Harry picked up the letters and opened the first one casually.

As he did so, he realised that the others were from two attractive ladies to whom he was paying court.

He had thought they would notice he had not called on them for several days and he realised with a twinkle in his eye, that he now had proof of it.

It was only as he drew the letter he was opening from its envelope that he realised that it came from France.

Then he saw to his astonishment that beneath an impressive crest which was surmounted by a coronet was an address which read: *Château de Bantôme*.

Canéda had risen from the table to help herself to some freshly picked mushrooms from the country, cooked in cream.

It was only after she had turned round that she saw the surprise on her brother's face and realised that he was reading a letter with, for him, unusual concentration.

He finished it and as she sat down at the table he flung the letter across to her saying:

"If that does not make you laugh, nothing will."

"Who is it from?" Canéda enquired.

"You will not believe it," Harry replied, "but it is from Mama's relations! How dare they, after all these years write to me, just because I have come into a title? It makes me want to spit!"

He spoke so derisively that Canéda laughed.

At the same time she picked up the letter from the table and read it with interest.

It was written in French, which because she was bilingual, she had no need to translate into English.

In a firm, authoritative hand someone had transcribed:

Château de Bantôme.

My dear Grandson:

It is with great pleasure that your Grandfather and I have learned that You have inherited the Earldom of Langstone and are now the Head of such a distinguished Family.

We think it is in the interests of both our families that the silence between Us should end, and that You should become acquainted not only with Your older Relatives like your Grandfather and Myself, but also with Your young Cousins, Hélène and Armand, who are very anxious to visit England.

It is time for Hélène, who is eighteen, to make her curtsy to Her Majesty the Queen, and for Armand to attend a levée held by the Prince of Wales. But of course, it would be much more pleasant for them if They had Your support.

But first Your Grandfather and I would like to extend to You an invitation to visit Us here to meet the surviving members of the great, historic Family of Bantôme, to which You belong.

We would of course be delighted if Your Sister could accompany You, and We will do everything in Our power to make Your visit as pleasant as possible.

I remain, in anticipation of a favourable reply,

Your Grandmother, who unfortunately You have never met.

Eugenie de Bantôme.

As she finished reading the letter Canéda gave a little gasp.

"You are right, Harry. It is unbelievable!" she said. "After ignoring Mama as if she had been swept off the face of the earth, how dare our Grandmother write such a

19

letter! I have never heard such cheek."

"I agree it is a damned impertinence on their part!" Harry exclaimed.

"Mama told me once," Canéda said in a low voice, "that when you were born she wrote to her mother telling her that she had a son, because she thought it would please her."

"I can guess what happened," Harry answered. "There was no reply."

"Worse than that, the letter was returned unopened."

"That is what I might have expected. So how do they dare write to us now, just because our circumstances have changed? I suppose if Papa had been an Earl when he eloped with Mama they might have forgiven her for chucking the *Duc*."

"I hate them!" Canéda cried. "Sometimes when Mama used to talk to me about her childhood I knew how home-sick she was and how much she longed to see not only her friends again, but also the Dordogne."

"I know," Harry agreed. "She loved it."

"She used to talk of the river and the Castles which gave it, she said, a fairy-like appearance. She used to make it sound so romantic that I longed to see it. But I never thought, because Papa was barred from France, that I would ever have the chance."

"I was the damned *Duc's* fault," Harry said. "When Papa who had visited France ever since he had been a small boy found he was no longer able to go there, it hurt him."

Canéda sighed.

"They certainly paid the price for running away with each other, but I do not think they ever regretted it."

"No, of course not," Harry agreed. "I have never seen two people as happy as Papa and Mama, and I only hope when I get married I shall be half as happy."

"That is exactly what I think too," Canéda said, "so you will understand that, whatever Aunt Anne says, I cannot marry Lord Warrington or any of those other stupid young men who have nothing better to do than to try to steal a kiss!"

Harry laughed.

"You ought to feel flattered!"

"Well, I do not!" Canéda said. "When I do marry, I want a very different kind of man from any of those I have met so far."

"Let me know when you find him," Harry said. "I do not mind telling you that the aunts are complaining that you are getting yourself talked about, and it is something of which they most ardently disapprove."

Canéda shrugged her shoulders in a gesture that was indisputably French.

"I cannot help it if men fall in love with me," she said, "and I knew Aunt Anne was furious last night because I had been so long in the Conservatory. But short of screaming for help I do not know how I could have got away from Lord Warrington any more quickly than I eventually managed to do."

"Shall I tell him to behave himself?" Harry asked.

"I do not believe it would do any good," Canéda replied. "The only thing is that I find it such a bore having him follow me around like a dog. Perhaps we could get away from London and him."

"What are you suggesting?" Harry asked. "That we should go to Langstone Park, or even to France?"

Canéda did not reply and he said:

"That is certainly one place in which I will never set foot, except that I would just like to tell my Grandmother and Grandfather and all the other Bantômes exactly what I think of them!"

He made an exclamation of anger and went on:

"How dare they treat Mama as they did, cutting her off as if she were a leper! As for the *Duc*, however much he felt insulted, he had no right to try to ostracise Papa in Paris and in London. I wish I could give him a taste of his

21

own medicine."

"I expect he is dead by now," Canéda replied. "He was much older than Mama and he wished to marry her because his wife was dead and he wanted a young woman to give him more children."

"That is the sort of reason one would expect," Harry said scornfully. "If his son or whoever has inherited the title, ever comes to England I will take my revenge and make it a pretty sharp one."

Canéda did not answer. She stared at the letter as if she were reading it again.

Suddenly she exclaimed:

"Harry, I have an idea!"

"What is it?"

"I think I might accept this invitation to go to France."

"Are you mad?" he asked. "Why on earth should you want to do that after the way they behaved to Mama?"

"It is because they behaved to Mama the way they did that, like you, I want to teach them a lesson," Canéda replied.

"I do not understand. What are you intending to do?" Harry asked.

"There is something I heard someone say at the party last week," Canéda said. "I did not pay much attention at the time and I must find out more about it, but I have a feeling that those who live in the Dordogne region of France are suffering financial losses."

Harry stared at her.

"Are you saying that the *Comtes* de Bantôme may have lost their money?"

"I do not know," Canéda answered. "It would explain would it not? – now that they know you are rich, why they are trying to patch up the differences between us. And perhaps they want Cousin Hélène to marry an Englishman."

"I do not believe it! It is too far fetched!" Harry said. "But if that is what they want, then you should certainly refuse to help them."

"I am not going to help them, stupid!" Canéda replied. "If I go to Bantôme I shall go, not as an ordinary lady-like member of the family, but as Lady Canéda, very rich and grand, and when I have made them thoroughly envious I will make it very clear that we would not lift a little finger to help them."

"It sounds quite an idea if you can be certain they have fallen on hard times," Harry agreed. "From all Mama used to tell me, they were rich and powerful and sitting with their vineyards on banks of gold."

"Yes, I know," Canéda said, "but supposing the vineyards became not so productive? What would happen then?"

"Your guess is as good as mine," Harry replied, "but if you take my advice, you will stay at home. Not even to avoid Warrington would I make the trip to France."

"It is no hardship," Canéda said in a dreamy voice, "I have always longed to see the country to which Mama belonged, and with which half of my blood has an undeniable affinity."

Harry did not reply and she went on:

"I read every book about France that ever comes my way, and all I can tell you is that, while I long to see Paris, I want, more than anything else in the world, to visit the parts of France that Mama described to me: the Dordogne, of course, which was her own country, and the Loire Valley, where she would have lived if she had married the *Duc*."

"She used to talk about him sometimes," Harry said, "and about his great Châteaux, and how wonderful the others were – Chenonceaux, Chambord, Chaumont, and of course Saumac where she would have lived with all the grandeur of a *Duchesse*."

"Let us go there," Canéda begged suddenly. "We can feast our eyes on what we have always wanted to see, and at the same time, wreak our vengeance on the Bantômes,

23

and if possible the *Duc* de Saumac as well."

"And leave all this?" Harry asked. "You must be raving! Do you think I would really leave Langstone at the moment and all the fun I am having in London?"

Canéda smiled.

"I grant you she is very alluring."

Harry grinned.

"That is what I find, and I assure you there are several men only too ready to step into my shoes."

"Then I might, I just might, go to France alone," Canéda said reflectively.

"You will do nothing of the sort!" her brother replied sharply. "You know as well as I do that you have to be chaperoned."

"I was not suggesting that," Canéda answered. "I meant if you would not come with me, I know exactly who would accompany me, if I asked her to do so."

"Who?"

"*Madame* de Goucourt!"

There was silence for a moment. Then Harry said:

"I do not doubt she would go anywhere if we were paying for her. But quite frankly, Canéda, I think this is a mad idea! Let us tear up the letter and leave them wondering if we have ever received it, or keep them on tenter-hooks for a little while at any rate."

He paused to add:

"If those damned cousins come here I swear I will do everything I can to make their visit a fiasco."

"I doubt if you will succeed," Canéda said. "My way is far cleverer and very subtle, and would be the direct answer to the way they treated Mama after she left them. She even had a little money of her own which her father arranged through his Lawyers she could not have unless she lived in France. It was an illegal action, but Papa could not afford the legal fees to fight it."

"So they literally stole Mama's money from her, and kept it all these years! I agree with you, they are despicable," Harry said. "But what is the point of torturing yourself by going to meet them?"

"I want revenge as much as you do, if not more," Canéda said, "and I am just wondering how I can revenge myself on the *Duc*. He is dead, but I suppose his son, if he had one, will have inherited his position. Perhaps I could make him miserable in one way or another."

"You had much better enjoy yourself in England."

"If I go I will not be gone for long," Canéda replied. "May I use your yacht?"

Harry threw out his hands in what was a slightly un-English gesture.

"I have not seen it yet, but of course it is yours to command."

"Thank you, dearest. I hope it is very large. I shall be taking carriage-horses with me, out-riders and of course, Ariel."

"Oh, for Heaven's sake!" Harry exclaimed. "The whole idea is crazy and I warn you, you are not setting foot outside this house without being properly chaperoned. So if *Madame* de Goucourt says 'No' – no it is!"

"But *Madame* de Goucourt will say 'Yes'," Canéda replied. "I am going to get in touch with her this morning. She lives in a small, uncomfortable little house in an unfashionable part of London, now that the glorious days when her husband was the French Ambassador have ended."

"She knew Mama and loved her," Harry said, "so I trust her to look after you."

Canéda did not contradict him, but there was a glint of mischief in the depths of her blue eyes which her brother did not see.

* * * * * *

Madame de Goucourt's house was, as Canéda had said, small and slightly shabby in a narrow-street off a fashionable Square.

The Frenchwoman had been much younger than her

25

husband the Ambassador. She was now only just fifty and resented the fate which had swept her from her importance as a member of the Diplomatic Corps into virtual obscurity.

Her daughter had however married an Englishman and her younger son was still finishing his education at Oxford, so because she wanted to be near them she had stayed in England rather than return to her native land.

She had known Clémentine de Bantôme ever since they were children and she had always been deeply sympathetic over the way she had been treated.

"It is not as if your husband is not of noble birth," she would say indignantly. "He belongs to a very distinguished English family, and although he has no money he is, *Ma Chérie,* a man from whom I can understand having once given him your heart, you could not take it back."

"That is true," Clémentine Lang had smiled. "I love Gerald, and I am the happiest woman in the whole world. But sometimes, just sometimes, Yvonne, I long to hear French voices, to eat French food, and to see the river, blue as the sky above it, winding its way through the vineyards and the deep gorges which as a child I was certain contained prehistoric animals!"

Madame de Goucourt had laughed.

"I understand how you feel," she said, "but you have your husband and those two adorable children."

"You do not suppose I have ever regretted running away, do you?" Clémentine and inquired. "It was the luckiest and most marvellous day of my life! But I can never forgive the *Duc* de Saumac for what he did to Gerald."

"That I can understand," *Madame* de Goucourt said. "It was cruel and wicked, but then he was a very strange man."

It seemed to *Madame* now that the years rolled back and it was not Canéda sitting in her small Sitting-Room, asking her questions, but Clémentine.

"Tell me about the *Duc* de Saumac, *Madame,*" Canéda asked.

"*Mon Dieu!* What makes you think of him, my little one? I thought you had come here to tell me about your successes in the *Beau Monde.* Everyone is talking about you, and how beautiful, intelligent and charming you are, and, as for Harry, all the ladies are wild about him."

"I know that," Canéda answered, "and it is very exciting for both of us after having lived so quietly for so long. But, please, *Madame,* answer my question about the *Duc* de Saumac."

"What is there to tell you?"

"Tell me about the old one...the one who was so cruel to Papa."

"Oh, he is dead, and I dare say not mourned by many people. As I expect you know, he wanted to marry your mother because having only one son by his wife who was ill for many, many years, he wanted when he was nearly sixty to start a new family, just in case anything should happen to his heir."

"And did anything happen to him?" Canéda enquired.

"No, he is now the *Duc* de Saumac, and let me see – he must be at least thirty-two or thirty-three years old."

"And in good health, I suppose," Canéda said a little bitterly.

"*He* is," *Madame* de Goucourt replied.

"Why should you say it like that?" Canéda enquired.

"Because in a way, it is very sad. His wife went mad soon after he was married. He was very young and had, in fact, just come of age."

"She went mad?" Canéda repeated to herself, and there was just a note of satisfaction in her voice.

"It was, of course, hidden away as it always is in France," *Madame* de Goucourt said, "but it must have been very bitter for the old *Duc* to realise there was no likelihood of his daughter-in-law producing any children, not even one, as he had managed to have himself."

27

"Well, I am delighted he was upset!" Canéda said.

"I believe the present *Duc* is a strange man," *Madame* de Goucourt continued, as if she spoke to herself.

"In what way?" Canéda enquired.

"Well, apparently he is very upset and sensitive about his wife's condition, and he withdrew from Society to live all the time at his Castle on the Loire. He runs a Riding-School there in which he trains horses for the Cavalry Regiments, and of course, for his own pleasure."

"A Riding-School!" Canéda exclaimed.

"He is, I believe, quite famous by now in that part of France," *Madame* de Goucourt said. "General Bourgueil when I last saw him was talking about it and saying what excellent horses his officers were able to obtain from the de Saumac School."

Canéda was silent for a moment. Then she drew the letter that Harry had received from the Château de Bantôme from her bag and gave it to *Madame* de Goucourt.

"Read this," she said.

Madame de Goucourt took it from her and holding up a pair of very elegant lorgnettes read it carefully.

When she finished she gave a little cry.

"This is extraordinary! Quite extraordinary!" she exclaimed. "Was not your brother surprised to receive it?"

"He was indeed," Canéda replied, "and so was I!"

Then as if she could not contain herself any longer she said angrily:

"How dare they write to us just because Harry has inherited the title and is now of some importance! Why did they not ask us to stay when Mama was alive? You know how she was never a person to bear a grudge. She would have forgiven them and it would have made her so happy."

There was just a little throb in Canéda's voice which told *Madame* de Goucourt how deeply she felt for her mother having been exiled from her kith and kin for so long.

"It is impossible to undo the past, *Ma Chérie,*" she said softly. "But if you can patch up the feud, you could perhaps make these people happy before they die."

"Make them happy?" Canéda cried. "I hate them and Harry hates them to! But I have an idea how I might make them really penitent and really ashamed at the way they behaved."

Madame de Goucourt put down her lorgnette and looked at Canéda in surprise.

"What are you saying?" she asked. "What are you suggesting?"

"First of all," Canéda answered, "I want you to tell me why, at this particular moment, apart from the fact that Harry is now important in England, they should have written to us."

There was a moment's hesitation and Canéda said insistently:

"I want the truth, *Madame.* I feel there is something behind it, and I want to know what it is."

"Of course, I cannot be certain," *Madame* said slowly, after a moment, "but there have been reports of trouble in the Dordogne."

"What sort of trouble?"

"First of all their harvests have been bad and my friends tell me that locally grown wheat cannot compete with cheaper American wheats which are imported and have depressed the prices of the French."

She paused and Canéda watching the expression on her face asked:

"And what else?"

For a moment she thought *Madame* de Goucourt would not tell her. Then she said:

"I have heard, although it is only a rumour, that phylloxera has affected a great number of vines in the region."

"Phylloxera!" Canéda exclaimed.

She would not have been her mother's daughter if she had not known something about the wine-growing which had been so essentially a part of Clémentine de Bantôme's youth and which was so important to France.

Gerald Lang had always appreciated French wines and he had taught his children to recognise the good ones, while their mother had explained how the greatest wines of France came from the Dordogne region.

Phylloxera was, as Canéda knew, the greatest disaster that could occur to any vineyard, and the insect itself was dreaded as other countries dreaded the plague.

Phylloxera had been introduced into France on an infected stock from America in the early 1860s.

Clémentine Lang had read about it in the newspapers and it had not been difficult for her family to understand how tragic she thought it was.

It was the French newspapers which their mother occasionally received from English friends who visited France, or French friends like *Madame* de Goucourt who knew how much she treasured them, which told her what was happening.

With phylloxera the vines lost their leaves and died, and it was a little while before it was discovered that the phylloxera aphid had affected the roots of the vine.

What was frightening was that by the time the dead vines were dug up and inspected the insects had moved on to other plants which above ground appeared to be unaffected and which the vine-growers therefore were loth to uproot.

"It is very, very dangerous for the vineyards," her mother had said, after she had read aloud what was in the newspaper.

"What does it matter to us who are not even allowed to look at the vines?" her husband had asked bitterly. "Although, thank God, there still seems to be a great deal of good Burgundy and claret in England!"

Clémentine had therefore said nothing more, but Canéda, because she was so close to her mother, realised she was worrying and she thought it pathetic that after all these years of being exiled by her family, she still worried over their possessions, especially the vineyards on which their fortune was based.

Privately she had thought in her heart that it would teach them a lesson if they suddenly became poor like her father and mother, and now from what *Madame* de Goucourt had said, she thought that was exactly what had happened.

"What you are saying," she said aloud, "is that the stuck-up *Comte* de Bantôme, my grandfather, needs Harry's and my help to launch his grandchildren into the Social World. And what of the help they gave us when we needed it?"

"I can understand that you feel bitter, Canéda," *Madame* de Goucourt said softly, "and I knew how much your mother minded, even when she was so happy, that she was isolated from her own people. We French are very close to each other, and the family means a great deal to us."

She paused before she went on:

"Although your mother was the happiest woman I have ever known in my life, I think sometimes she longed with one part of her for the closeness of her parents, her brothers, her sisters, and of course their children, some of whom will be about the same age as yourself."

She paused again.

"The de Bantômes are a very large family, and I think you would enjoy knowing them, and they you."

"They are not going to know me, except as an avenging angel," Canéda answered, "and because that is what I intend to be, I want your help, *Madame*."

"My help?" *Madame* de Goucourt asked in astonishment.

"It is quite simple," Canéda replied. "I want you to come with me to France."

She saw a sudden light come into the Frenchwoman's eyes which told her the invitation would not be refused.

Then she added:

"I intend, *Madame*, to teach not only the de Bantômes a lesson, but if it is possible the *Duc* de Saumac one as well, and one he will never forget!"

CHAPTER TWO

With its white sails billowing out in the wind the *Sea-Gull* nosed its way slowly into the port of St. Nazaire.

Canéda had been on deck since dawn as they sailed past Belle Ile into the harbour.

She was so excited that she had found it almost impossible to sleep since she had left Folkestone. It was there that the late Earl's yacht had been moored in order always to be ready to carry its owner across the Channel any time he wished to go.

She was certain that Harry would soon avail himself of this new toy, but there were so many other distractions among his possessions that he had been quite content for Canéda to see and use the *Sea-Gull* first.

The *Sea-Gull* had been commissioned by their uncle only three years before he died and therefore was of the most up-to-date design. To Canéda's delight there was plenty of room to carry quite a number of horses, besides a travelling-chariot.

She had been a little apprehensive lest the sea should be rough and the horses upset, especially Ariel, but Ben who was in charge had been very reassuring.

"Now ye leave it to me, Miss Canéda – I means M'Lady!" he said. "T'horses'll be all right – I'll see t' that."

Canéda knew he meant what he said and there was no doubt that Ben was a wizard when it came not only to training the horses, but to looking after them.

She had been fourteen when she had rushed into her father's Study to tell him that there was news of a Circus coming to the small market town which was only two miles from where they lived.

"We must see it, Papa! You must take me to the Circus!" Canéda had cried.

"I hate to see wild animals in captivity," Gerald Lang had replied.

"It is not the wild animals I want to see," Canéda answered, "but a poster hanging up in the village says there is a performing horse who will obey every command she is given which makes her the cleverest animal in the world."

Gerald Lang had looked sceptical, but because Canéda was so insistent he promised to take her to the Circus.

He knew exactly the tumbledown show it would be, consisting of a few mangy old horses, some clowns who were not very funny, a Ringmaster who doubtless owned the Circus and drank away his financial troubles and, if they were fortunate, a couple of acrobats.

But he was well aware that for Canéda living very quietly in the country especially with Harry away at School, it would be a delight that would rival Ashley's Circus in London.

Clémentine Lang said she was too busy in the house to accompany them, but father and daughter had set off.

They travelled in the old-fashioned gig which Gerald Lang drove with an expertise and a flourish that made Canéda aware that he should have had an up-to-date chaise with two or even four superlative horses.

The gig had been the only form of transport they could afford, but as far as she was concerned she was so happy to be with her father that nothing else mattered.

They reached the small town and Gerald Lang saw there was the usual collection of farmers' wives selling their wares in the market-place with the townsfolk taking a long time to make up their minds whether they should buy an old hen suitable for boiling or a more expensive fat chicken to roast.

There were turnips, beets and cabbages brought in from the countryside, pats of golden butter, honeycomb and inevitably rabbits and hares that had been trapped or snared, regardless of what time of year it was.

Canéda was not interested in the market which stood in the centre of the town.

She was waiting breathlessly for her father to drive to where in the field that sloped down to the river the Circus had been erected.

There was a big tent which let in the rain in bad weather and there was a sawdust ring with rows of rickety seats round it.

They had travelled for too many months without repair and were likely to precipitate those who sat on them at any unexpected moment, to the ground.

There was a Band playing and to Canéda the Ringmaster in his red coat, top-hat and cracking his long whip, was very impressive as he introduced his performers to an audience that consisted mostly of gaping children, a few farm-hands and some giggling girls.

The first turn was quite ordinary, at least to Gerald Lang and consisted of four grey horses with feathers on their bridles and ballerinas perched precariously on their backs.

He thought the horses looked as old as their riders, and there was certainly not much skill in raising a leg above a frilly ballet-skirt while holding tightly onto the front of the saddle.

But Canéda's small face was rapt with enjoyment and Gerald Lang said nothing but watched his daughter rather than the performers.

The clowns made her laugh, and there was an acrobatic turn which made her hold her breath.

Then the Ringmaster announced:

"Now, Ladies and Gentlemen, you'll see the most sensational, the most intelligent, the must unusual horse in the world. Her name is Juno and she understands every word that is said to her. She also can dance in a manner that no other horse has been able to do in all my long

35

experience of them."

There was applause from the crowd as Juno came into the ring.

She was black with a white star on her nose and Gerald Lang saw that she had once undoubtedly been a very fine mare, but was now getting old.

Riding her was a small jockey with an ugly, impudent face, a disarming grin and twinkling eyes. He made her perform as if she was a musical instrument in the hands of a master of the art.

Juno waltzed in time to the Band, then she danced the polka which had just become fashionable. She walked on her hind legs, answered questions by shaking or nodding her head.

Finally when jumps had been erected round the ring, Juno sailed over them in a style that made Canéda clap her hands wildly at such a brilliant performance.

The enthusiastic applause of everyone in the big tent made her rider decide that she should take the jumps once again and now with a roll of the drums she started off, taking each fence in a way which made her seem almost to fly through the air.

Quite suddenly when she reached the last fence of all she rose from the ground, seemed to stagger, and the next moment, almost before anyone could realise what was happening, she crashed down on the other side of the fence in a crumpled heap.

There was a scream from the women in the audience, a groan from the men, and Canéda clutched at her father's hand.

"What is happening, Papa?"

"Her heart, I should imagine," Gerald Lang replied.

"Oh, she cannot die!" Canéda cried. "Please, Papa, see if there is anything you can do. I could not bear that beautiful horse to die in such a manner."

Because Gerald Lang knew only too well what his daughter was feeling, they went round to the back of the tent as Juno was dragged out of the ring and the clowns went on to take the audience's mind off the tragedy.

There were one or two grooms besides the small man who had been riding her when Gerald Lang and Canéda reached them, but it was obvious at first glance that there was nothing anyone could do for the mare.

Juno was dead, because her heart, as Gerald Lang had rightly suspected, had given out.

Canéda crouched down beside the mare and as she did so she saw the small jockey who had been riding her in his gaudy theatrical costume, was kneeling on the other side.

He was crying unashamedly, tears running down his ugly, lined face, and his despair was in itself very moving.

"I am sorry," Canéda said softly.

"Her were a wonderful 'orse!"

"Have you been with her long?" Canéda enquired.

"For ten years, Miss," he replied. "I started to train 'er with 'er first master and when 'e dies 'e gives 'er to me. Her were mine, me very own."

"I know what you must be feeling," Canéda said softly, "and there is nothing I can say, except that I am so very sorry for you."

She could understand that he was desolate in losing such a magnificent horse and one who was so clever.

"I've got sommat to show ye, Miss, if ye'd come with I," the man said.

"Yes, of course", Canéda agreed.

He rose to his feet and as she rose too, she found her father standing beside her.

"He has something to show us, Papa," she said, slipping her hand into his.

Gerald Lang nodded but did not speak. With his daughter he followed the jockey with his red and gold braided coat until they came to a battered tent where all the horses who worked for the Circus had been housed.

The grays were already back tethered to posts, but still wearing their feathers on the front of their bridles as they

37

would be wanted in the finale. But there was one end of the tent shut off from the rest which appeared at first to be empty until, as the jockey walked into it Canéda saw something moving.

It was then she was aware of what he had brought her to see. It was a foal of about six or seven weeks old, and already showing the good breeding of its mother.

As Canéda stroked its neck it nuzzled its black nose against her, and she heard her father say:

"What are you going to do now?"

"I don't know, Sir, an' that's the truth," the little man answered. "Juno were me living, so to speak, and it'll be a year or two afore I can do anythin' with Ariel and that'll be too soon for most Circuses to be interested in 'im."

There was something both helpless and hopeless in the way he spoke and Canéda suddenly knew what she wanted.

She rose, moved closer to her father and putting her hand on his arm looked up at him with pleading eyes.

"Please…Papa."

She knew even as she spoke that he was thinking they could not afford it, and yet because she knew instinctively that it was not only what she wanted, but what would please him too, she said again:

"Please…"

Gerald Lang was well aware that the old groom who had looked after his horses ever since he had been married was past working, and should have been retired ages ago.

He had, however, been afraid of what a younger man might cost him, and he had already discussed with his wife how they could afford to pension off the old groom and pay someone to take his place.

But he could not bear to refuse his daughter and he knew how much the foal could mean to her when she had few amusements and little companionship when Harry was away at School.

"Supposing for the time being," he said to the small

man beside him who still had tears on his cheeks, "you and Ariel come and stay in my stables. That will give you time to get over the death of Juno and think about your future."

"D'you mean that, Sir?"

"I mean it, and we will be expecting you later tonight, or tomorrow morning."

The expression of gratitude and relief on the little man's face was pathetic.

"Me name's Ben, Sir, an' your kindness be sommat I'll n'er forget."

Only when they had left the Circus after giving Ben directions how to get to the Manor did Canéda say nervously:

"You do think he will come? Supposing he wants to stay with the Circus?"

"I have a feeling he will come," her father answered.

"I feel the same. I will look after Ariel and leave Ben plenty of time to see to your horses.

"Of course," her father replied. "That is part of the bargain."

Canéda put her cheek against his arm.

"Thank you, thank you," she said. "How can I ever thank you enough for being so kind?"

"I am just wondering what your mother will say," Gerald Lang replied a little ruefully.

Clémentine had understood.

She could never bear to see people suffering, and when Canéda told her how Ben had cried she had known it would have been impossible for her husband and daughter to walk away without trying to help.

Ben had arrived with Ariel, and without his theatrical clothes he had seemed strange and insignificant.

He may have been small, but the Langs found he was immensely strong. He never seemed to tire and he never appeared to stop working.

Gerald Lang had never had his horses groomed better

or looked after in the way that could not have been improved on even if they had been in the finest stables in England.

What was more, from the very first Ben seemed to settle down and make the place his home almost as if he had been born there.

And as for Ariel, words would fail Canéda every time she thought of him.

He grew prodigiously in the first year, changing from a small foal into a beautiful creature who looked as if he had stepped straight out of mythology.

He had beautiful lines, a fine head and a coat which seemed to shine as if it was made of polished ebony.

He grew and grew, and by the time he was two years old, one of the sights of the countryside was to see Canéda looking very small but very lovely, riding an enormous black stallion that appeared too spirited for her to handle.

But from the moment Canéda and Ben came together they started to teach Ariel the same tricks that had made his mother Juno so extraordinary, and a great many more.

Ariel would obey both Canéda and Ben, and they would vie with each other in thinking up new things for him to do, teaching him not by threats or through fear, but with love.

Sometimes Canéda felt as if Ariel thought up his own tricks to do and was ready to perform them almost before she had been able to explain to him what she wanted.

"He understands, he really understands!" she would say to Ben who would scratch his head and say:

"Animals, Miss Canéda, can be a sight cleverer than most folk, especially 'orses like Ariel and Juno."

The little man had loved Juno, and Canéda suspected he sometimes cried at night because he missed her so.

She often felt a little guilty because she had the feeling that Ariel preferred her to Ben, and she had taken him away from him.

But Ben put her right on this. One day she said to him:

"You are happy here, Ben? You would never leave us, would you?"

There was a touch of anxiety in her voice because she felt afraid Ben might want to go roaming again, and it would break her heart to lose Ariel.

But Ben had nodded his head.

"I be happy, Miss Canéda, 'cos yer father, yer mother and ye treats I as one of th' family. Ye've made this a home for I as you have for Ariel, an' that's all any man could ask."

When Canéda had told her mother what Ben had said, she had answered:

"Ben is a dear little man, and he is good. No-one could have the control over a horse that he has and not be a good man. Animals, especially horses, sense better than we can what a man is like in his soul."

It was Ben who had chosen which horses, which grooms, and which out-riders should accompany Canéda on her trip to France.

Harry, who also looked on Ben as one of the family, had taken him aside to say:

"You will look after Her Ladyship, and see that she does not get into any trouble?"

"I'll do that, M'Lord," Ben promised.

"I do not approve of her going off on this wild-goose-chase," Harry went on, "but she has set her heart on it, and so I have agreed. But if anything goes wrong, you are to bring her home immediately. Do you understand, Ben?"

"I understands, M'Lord," Ben replied, "and 'Er Ladyship won't come to no harm if I can 'elp it."

"I trust you, Ben," Harry said, putting his hand on the little man's shoulder

* * * * * *

The yacht with the wind in her sails was moving slowly but surely into the harbour as Ben came up to join Canéda.

"We have made it, Ben," Canéda said, a note of

satisfaction in her voice.

"Yus, I knows, M'Lady. What now?"

"When we have got the horses off and the carriage ready we will set off for Nantes, where we will stay the night."

"Very good, M'Lady."

"We will be riding, if not today," Canéda replied, "certainly tomorrow."

She smiled as she spoke and Ben smiled back.

"It's just what Ariel be a-waiting for, M'Lady, a good gallop. 'T'll take the stiffness out of 'is legs."

"He is all right?" Canéda asked quickly.

"Right as rain, M'Lady, so don't ye worry about 'im. A little hardship never hurt a 'orse as long as 'e ain't frightened."

Canéda knew that none of the horses on the yacht had been frightened by the roughness of the sea, simply because Ben had been with them, calming them.

She was quite certain he had stayed with them all night, sleeping below so that he was there ready to soothe them at the slightest whimper.

She thought once again how lucky she was to have Ben, and as if he knew what she was thinking, he said:

"Now don't ye worrit, M'Lady, everythin's fine, an' there's nothing for ye to do but enjoy yerself."

Canéda was only too willing to obey.

France, as she drove along beside *Madame* de Goucourt, was exactly as she had thought it would be.

The wide open countryside, the green banks of the Loire, and rising ahead of them the towers and spires of Nantes.

They stayed the night at an ancient Inn where the beds were made of the softest goose-feathers and the food was gastronomic.

The Proprietor and his buxom wife were obviously extremely impressed by the elegance of their guests and the largeness of their entourage.

It was only when *Madame* de Goucourt and Canéda had finished dining in the comfortable private room and the Landlord had bowed his way out that *Madame* said:

"Well, *Ma Chéri*, you are in France, but you have still not told me why we have disembarked at St. Nazaire rather than Bordeaux. As you are well aware, at this moment we should be staying somewhere beside the Dordogne rather than the Loire."

Canéda gave a little smile which told *Madame* de Goucourt without words that she was plotting something.

"Now, Canéda, I have been given strict instructions by Harry to look after you," she said. "You know as well as I do that he expected us to stay just for a short time with your grandparents, then return home. Therefore I ask you again — why are we here?"

"I have a plan, *Madame,* but I do not wish to talk about it in case it does not come off. All I can beg you, is not to ask me too many questions. Let me play my cards my own way."

Madame de Goucourt laughed.

"I am well aware you are up to something, Canéda," she said, "but because I am so grateful to you for bringing me back to my beloved country and for spoiling me by giving me such elegant gowns in which to dazzle my friends and relatives when I meet them, I cannot command, but only beg you not to do anything outrageous."

Canéda tilted her head a little to one side.

"It depends what you call outrageous, *Madame*," she replied. "Shall I say I am taking justice into my own hands, rather than waiting for it to work by chance?"

"Oh, Canéda, Canéda!" *Madame* de Goucourt cried, "you make me very apprehensive. But because I am tired I intend to take a soothing tisane and retire to bed, hoping that tomorrow I shall not be in a terrible state of anxiety and worry."

"You will be neither, *Madame*," Canéda said reassuringly. "And you did say you had some friends who live near Angers."

"Yes, indeed," *Madame* de Goucourt replied, "some old friends who it will give me great happiness to see again. They are not very rich or fashionable, you understand, and therefore you might find them rather dull, but I could not come to this part of France without seeing them."

"That is what I thought," Canéda said with satisfaction, "and I promise you that you shall have plenty of time with your friends, while I shall be with mine."

It was only the next day when they were driving along the side of the Loire through the most beautiful country towards Angers that *Madame* de Goucourt said:

"Do you realise, Canéda, that you have not told me the name of the friends you intend to visit?"

"I do not think you would know them," Canéda replied, "and I want, *Madame*, to ask you a favour."

"But of course," *Madame* de Goucourt replied.

"Do not tell your friends too much about me," Canéda said. "It will only make them curious, and for the moment I do not want anyone in this part of world to know who I am."

Madame de Goucourt looked at her in utter astonishment.

"Are you telling me that I am not to say I am accompanied by Lady Canéda Lang?"

"Please, I beg you not to mention my name," Canéda pleaded. "If you need to make any explanation for the carriage and the horses, you could say that you have been loaned them by a rich English nobleman. After all, no-one would be surprised at that, and they will naturally assume that it is a Beau who has been so generous."

Madame de Goucourt laughed.

"You are frightening me! You are up to some monkey tricks which will make your brother very angry with me, and you will not be the only one to be in disgrace."

"Just trust me," Canéda begged.

Although *Madame* Goucourt pleaded with her, she refused to be drawn into a discussion or explanation as to what her plans for the future might be.

As *Madame's* friends were in straitened circumstances, Canéda refused to consider staying with them.

Instead they passed through Angers and found a delightful Inn a few miles outside the town situated on the North bank of the Loire.

Here too the Proprietor was exceedingly impressed by his visitors, and although Canéda privately thought the food was not as good as they had enjoyed the first night, the whole staff of the Inn tried to please and it was impossible to find fault.

Only after they had settled into their bedrooms and finished a meal in a private Sitting-Room did Canéda say to the Landlord:

"I wish to see my Head Groom before I retire to bed. Would you be kind enough to send for him?"

"Of course, *Madame*," the Inn-Keeper replied.

Madame de Goucourt rose to her feet from the comfortable chair in which she had been sitting.

"If you are going to talk horses, I shall retire to bed," she said. "Gossip about people I always enjoy, but I cannot acclimatise myself to a long and intensive conversation over the well-being of a horse."

Canéda laughed.

"Go to bed, *Madame*, and have your beauty sleep. Your friends must not think that Britain has aged you since you last met, which would definitely be an aspersion on our poor country."

"As it is at least six years since I have seen them, *Mon Amie*," *Madame* replied, "they will doubtless notice there are new lines around my eyes, and I am definitely stouter than I was when I was last here."

"Rubbish!" Canéda replied. "You look lovely, and you know it! After all, *Madame*, Mama always told me that while your husband was the Doyen of the Diplomatic

Corps you were undoubtedly the Belle of it!"

"You flatter me, child!" *Madame* de Goucourt said with satisfaction.

She kissed Canéda affectionately and went upstairs, leaving her alone in the small private room.

Canéda had not long to wait before there was a knock and Ben came in.

He was looking exceedingly smart in his well cut Langstone livery with its crested silver buttons and waist-coat of blue and yellow stripes.

The out-riders wore powdered wigs, but Ben had a high cockaded top-hat which he wore impudently on the side of his dark hair which was just beginning to turn grey.

He was holding it now in his hand, and he put it down on a chair near the door and stood waiting for Canéda's instructions.

"Are the horses all right, Ben?"

"Th' stables be satisfactory, M'Lady. I gets the lads to muck 'em out an' put down fresh straw. The 'orses'll have a good night, as we all will."

"While we are here there is something I want you to do for me, Ben."

The way Canéda spoke made the little man's eyes alert as if he knew already what she had to say was important.

"About two miles away on the other side of the river," Canéda began, "there is the Château de Saumac. It is what you and I would term a Castle. I have always been told that as it stands on a hill, you can see it from miles away, silhouetted against the sky-line."

Ben was listening and Canéda went on:

"The *Duc* de Saumac has a Riding-School in the small town beneath the Château. From which I have learnt there are some fine buildings attached to it where the Cavalry Officers stay when they bring their horses for schooling."

Ben nodded, but he did not speak and Canéda con-tinued:

"I was told in Nantes that there is a wall surrounding the outside grounds where the horses exercise, but this I want you to ascertain. Also to find out everything you can about when the *Duc* is in the School, what time he spends there supervising the jumping and how we can approach him."

"I understands, M'Lady."

"What is important is that no-one must know who you are."

"Ye mean that I'm not in yer employment, M'Lady?"

"I mean that you are to be just an interested stranger, and on no account must you mention my name. Moreover, and this must be remembered, Ben, none of our men are to talk about me to anybody."

She paused for a moment to let this sink in. Then she said:

"If anyone asks, you are employed by *Madame* de Goucourt. You are her servant and at her command Is that understood?"

"Yus, M'Lady."

"You have told me that you understand French since you came with the Circus to France."

"That be true."

"I will tell you what I intend to do once you have the information for me. But remember we definitely are English and not French in any way."

"That makes it easier for I, M'Lady."

It was obvious to Canéda that Ben was beginning to sense they were to be involved in an adventure.

She had often wondered if after the roving life he had lived with the Circus, going from place to place, having different problems and new difficulties day after day, he was not now sometimes a little bored.

Life in their Manor home had been very quiet with too few horses to look after, and nothing more exciting happening than to attend the nearest Hunt meeting, or accompany her father to the local Point-to-Point.

Ben had certainly welcomed the change in their circumstances, and had been thrilled and overwhelmed, as they all were, by the stables at Langstone, the horses Harry had inherited, and the new ones he immediately began to buy.

Although Ben said nothing, Canéda thought that what she was planning now would be an escapade after his own heart.

She knew he had half-guessed already what she intended from the instructions she had given him before they left England as to what he was to bring with him.

"How soon can you get me the information I enquire?" Canéda required.

"I'll get over t' Saumac at th' first light o' dawn, M'Lady. By the time ye're having yer breakfast I should be able to tell ye what ye wants to know."

"That is what I hoped you would say."

"Leave it t'me, M'Lady. I'll see that th' lads keep their mouths shut. They're a good lot and'll do what I tells 'em."

"I know that," Canéda replied, "and thank you, Ben. What I am planning I could not do with anyone else but you."

She liked his smile as his lips parted. Then he said:

"I be a-betting, M'Lady, ye've not told 'Is Lordship what's in the air?"

"Certainly not!" Canéda replied. "What the mind does not know, the heart does not grieve over. His Lordship thinks I am on the way to Bordeaux."

"We'll be going there, M'Lady?"

"Later," Canéda replied. "But the first thing is the assault on the Château de Saumac."

She spoke the last words almost beneath her breath but she thought that Ben had heard them judging by the way he grinned before he bade her goodnight.

When she was alone she drew a deep breath and told herself that everything was going well.

She had reached Angers and she would reach the Château de Saumac. The only difficulty was how to bring herself to the notice of the *Duc* and take the shortest time possible in achieving her revenge on him.

What *Madame* de Goucourt had told her about him made it seem less easy than it had when the idea had first come to her.

A recluse, a man embittered by the madness of his wife, was rather different from the ardent, eager admirers like Lord Warrington whom she had left behind in England.

Then she told herself there was one link that was more important than anything else – their love of horses.

No man could build a Riding-School and devote, from all she had heard, all his waking hours to horses without loving them.

At the same time, looking at the flaws in her plan, Canéda told herself that she knew very little about Frenchmen.

She might be half-French, but the men she had met since leaving School had all been English, and mostly, Canéda thought, very traditionally English at that.

What she wanted to know was the way to arouse a Frenchman's interest in her.

If books were to be believed, Frenchmen were always ready to pursue a pretty woman, and, if possible, to seduce her.

Canéda was not quite certain what this entailed, but she had read some of the ardent, passionate poems that had been amongst her mother's books.

She had also read a number of the French novels that French friends like *Madame* de Goucourt often loaned or gave to Clémentine Lang because they thought she should be *au fait* with what was being discussed in the Salons of Paris.

"Love to a Frenchman is very important," her mother had said once. "He thinks about beautiful women, he dreams about them, while the Englishman of the same age

49

is concerned mainly with sport, and of course horses."

"Papa loves you, Mama," Canéda had said.

Her mother had laughed.

"Yes, darling, that is true, but I sometimes feel I am being beaten to the winning-post by a horse!"

Her father had heard what she had said as he came into the room. He put his arms around her and turned her face up to his.

"Do you want me to show you that you mean more to me by promising that I will never ride again?" he asked.

"No, of course not!" his wife cried. "Just tell me that I come first in your heart, and that your four-legged loves are left well behind!"

"When you are running they do not even leave the starting-point," Gerald Lang replied.

He kissed his wife and when he released her Canéda had seen the flush on her mother's cheeks and the light in her eyes, and had known how happy she was.

But that had taught her very little about Frenchmen.

Then she tried to reassure herself that at least it would be a sporting effort.

She went to bed, but although it was exceedingly comfortable and she was tired, she found it difficult not to go over and over every detail of her plan once again.

She had been turning it over in her mind ever since she had decided to come to France, but she had known it would be a great mistake to say too much to Harry or even to *Madame* de Goucourt until it was too late for them to try to stop her.

Now she was actually here, two miles from the de Saumac Château, and she lay in the darkness wondering what the *Duc* was like.

"If the Château is barricaded against me," she told herself, "it will be in keeping with his his father's nasty, vindictive character."

She felt the anger she had always felt when she thought about the way the *Duc* had behaved blazing within her almost like an avenging fire.

"I have to make him suffer," she murmured, "and however much he does suffer it cannot make up for all that Papa suffered for over twenty years."

She fell asleep just before dawn and when the first light of the sun's rays threw a golden light on the slow moving Loire, Ben on one of the least noticeable horses they had brought with them, rode along the side of the river to where he had learned there was a bridge.

He arrived in Saumac just as the housewives were opening their doors and windows and streets sprang into activity with the merchants, the vendors and the sweepers starting the day.

Saumac was a small place with pretty gabled houses and an ancient Church, overshadowed by the huge Château soaring above it. The pointed turreted towers were silhouetted, as Canéda said they would be, against the sky.

It had been a fortress from which many battles had been fought at the end of the 16th century.

Now it looked more beautiful than formidable, and with the morning sunshine glinting on the long windows which had replaced the arrow slits of the original building, it had an elegance that was very different from what had been its war-like importance.

However, Ben's instructions did not concern the Château.

He found the Riding-School without difficulty. The buildings of which Canéda had spoken were an example of fine eighteenth century architecture and so were the stables attached to them.

Surrounding them was a high wall, built in a square and with only one gate which was of wood, ornamented with heavy iron hinges and a very formidable-looking lock.

Ben engaged the first passerby who seemed friendly in conversation.

"What's in there?" he enquired in his bad but understandable French.

"A school for horses," was the answer.

"Sounds interesting," Ben remarked, "I'd likes to see it."

The man to whom he was speaking shook his head.

"Ye can't do that."

"Why not?"

"*Monsieur le Duc* will not allow anyone in except those concerned with horses."

"No spectators?"

"Not often."

"B'ain't ye curious to see what goes on?"

"Horses don't interest me, *Monsieur*," was the reply, "only women!"

They both laughed, then Ben looked serious.

He rode several times round the huge square. Finally he found a tree which he could climb without difficulty and when he descended and mounted his horse again, he rode back the way he had come with a smile on his lips.

He had discovered what Canéda wanted to know.

CHAPTER THREE

The sun was reflected in the wide river and there was the freshness of the morning in the scent which came from the blossoming shrubs which bordered the road along which Canéda and Ben were riding.

She had crept out from the Hotel while *Madame* de Goucourt was still asleep, knowing that she would have been horrified at her appearance.

She had in fact spent a great deal of thought on choosing her habit which was certainly not one that a Lady of Quality would have worn in Rotten Row.

In fact it would have been too *outré* and extreme even for the Pretty Horse-Breakers who met at the Achilles statue to show off their mounts and themselves.

If Canéda had wished to be spectacular then she had certainly succeeded.

After changing her mind several times she had finally chosen a habit made of heavy silk, camellia pink in colour.

It was frogged with white braid and ornamented with large pearl buttons.

On her head the gauze veil which floated behind her was also pink, and the only other colour to complete the *ensemble* were the toes of her highly polished riding-boots which peeped from beneath her skirts, and her own dark hair.

That she looked lovely went without saying, but also very theatrical.

She accentuated this impression by reddening her lips with a different salve to that which she used sparingly on other occasions.

Her skin was so dazzlingly white that it did not really need the film of powder she had applied to it.

On Ariel's back she certainly looked striking, and it was fortunate that it was so early in the morning, otherwise she might easily have attracted a crowd.

She was complemented by Ben who, on her instructions, was wearing the red, lavishly gold-braided coat he had worn in the Circus.

His new cockaded hat set at an anle on his head needed no embellishment, his white breeches were smartly cut and his white gloves had been expensive.

He and Canéda had discussed at some length what horse he should ride for they had nothing with them to equal the appearance of Ariel.

Harry had recently purchased a black stallion with a white nose and four white fetlocks.

He had christened it 'Black Boy' and Canéda thought the horse added to their theatrical appearance.

They rode quickly and in silence.

Canéda going over in her mind all that Ben had told her of the Riding-School, was determined she would not make a mistake in anything she did, for she knew that everything depended on there not being a snag at the last moment.

Because she was apprehensive she could not help thinking that perhaps the *Duc* would decide not to attend the School this particular morning – or when she did appear, he would order her abruptly from the grounds.

Then she told herself that if she could command the attention, admiration and adoration of so many Englishmen, one Frenchman could not be so very different.

They crossed the bridge over the River Loire and Canéda looked ahead of them to where the Château de Saumac stood like a sentinel above the small town.

She thought there must be a magnificent panoramic view from its windows over the river and the valley, and she wondered if she would ever see it.

Then she told herself this was the moment when she must have complete and absolute confidence in herself in the knowledge that what she was doing was right and just.

When they had crossed the bridge she let Ben go ahead to lead her straght to the Riding-School.

They twisted their way through some small, attractive streets with old gabled houses.

Then suddenly, as she had expected, Canéda saw the high wall that Ben had described to her and at the far end large attractive buildings that had been built to house the Cavalry Officers.

Now was the moment when they must not waste time, for though there were only a few people moving about the streets, they stared at them in astonishment.

The last thing Canéda wanted was to collect a crowd who would perhaps get in the way.

Ben drew his horse to a standstill beneath a chestnut tree that was just coming into flower which Canéda guessed was the one from which he had observed the School yesterday.

He tied his reins to an adjacent railing and climbed agilely and with the expertise of a circus performer, up the tree without marking his clothes or making it seem any more difficult than taking an ordinary walk.

There was a moment when Canéda held her breath in case, as she feared, the *Duc* was not there.

Then Ben smiled and nodded his head, and she instantly moved Ariel back some distance from the wall and waited for Ben to give her the signal they had arranged.

As she felt a little nervous and was frightened that it might communicate itself to Ariel she bent forward to pat his neck with her gloved hand.

"Steady, boy! I am relying on you!" she said softly, and Ariel twitched his ears as if he understood what she was saying to him.

Then she heard Ben give a low whistle and rode forward.

The wall was high, but Ariel cleared it with several inches to spare, tucking his legs under him in the way Ben and Canéda had taught him to do over the jumps at Langstone.

He landed on the other side of the wall on sandy ground and Canéda, looking ahead, saw as she had expected a man standing in the centre of the School, astride what she knew was an exceptionally fine grey.

There was no time however to do more than recognise him from Ben's description for at the word of command, Ariel rose up on his hind legs and moved quite a way towards the *Duc* before he was back on four.

Then he waltzed round and round as Canéda had taught him to do.

It was the dance his mother had performed in the Circus and he reversed as she had done.

By now they were within ten feet of the *Duc* and Canéda pulled Ariel to a standstill. At her quietly whispered order he put out his front legs and bowed his head while Canéda sitting bolt upright in the saddle raised her jewel-handled whip in salute.

Now she could look directly at the *Duc* and he was not in the least what she had expected.

She thought he would be small, but he was large with square shoulders. He was dark, but not overwhelmingly so, and she had the idea that his eyes were grey.

She had expected him to look grim and perhaps, because everyone had said he was so reserved, secretive.

Instead he looked raffish and in fact there was almost a devil-may-care expression on his very handsome face, as if he defied the world and was derisive of anything it could offer him.

Ariel rose to his feet, and now Canéda and the *Duc* were facing each other, and for a moment there was silence.

Then the other riders who had drawn in their mounts to watch Canéda burst into applause and she had no time to notice any more.

They clapped enthusiastically and until they were finished there was no chance of either Canéda or the *Duc* speaking.

As if she took the appreciation as her due, Canéda smiled at them, bowing her head gracefully in first one direction, then the other. Then her eyes came back to the *Duc* and she looked at him questioningly as if she wondered why he too did not applaud what he must admit was an outstanding performance.

"Who are you?" he demanded.

"*Bonjour, Monsieur le Duc*," Canéda replied. 'I am delighted to make your acquaintance."

"In a somewhat unusual manner!" he remarked dryly.

"I may be wrong," Caneda replied, "but I rather doubted if your awe-inspiring gates would open for me, and I was so very anxious to meet you."

Her voice softened on the last words and she deliberately made her blue eyes seem flirtatious and inviting as she looked at him, then fluttered her dark eye-lashes.

"I asked you a question," the *Duc* said. "Who are you?"

"My name is Canéda."

There was a pause before he enquired:

"Is that all?"

"It is the name under which I perform.'"

For the first time there was a faint smile on his lips.

"So you belong to the Circus."

"A very superior one."

"That, of course, I would not doubt."

Again there was a pause before the *Duc* said:

"Well, *Mademoiselle*, now that you are here in a somewhat unconventional manner, what can I do for you?"

"That is what I hoped you would ask me, *Monsieur*. I want to know if there is anything you can teach me, anything that my horses do not know already."

She accentuated the plural and as she realised the *Duc*

had noticed it, she said:

"Perhaps you will allow my groom to join me. He has another horse I would like you to see, although he is not in the same class as Ariel."

"That is the name of your magnificent stallion?"

"Yes, I pronounce it in the English way."

Canéda smiled.

She felt with a little sense of triumph that the conversation was going exactly as she wished it to do.

"Perhaps I should explain, *Monsieur,* that when I am in England I am English, and in France I am French."

She thought he was puzzled, and explained:

"My mother was French, my father...so I have always been told...was English."

Again at the frankness of her words she saw a faint smile on the *Duc's* lips.

He had a hard mouth, she thought, it might even be a cruel one, but it was belied by the expression in his eyes that made her think he was what the mediaeval Knights must have looked like who warred so ferociously over France in previous centuries.

He lifted his hand and one of the men in uniform rode to his side.

"Have the gates opened for *Mademoiselle's* groom to join her," the *Duc* odered.

The Officer saluted and rode towards the gateway.

The *Duc* turned his face again towards Canéda.

"We appear to have something in common besides horse-flesh," he said. "You say you are half-French and half-English, and I am the same. Except my mother was English and my father French."

Canéda was both startled and intr'gued.

Not even *Madame* Goucourt had told her that the *Duc* had English blood in him, but it would certainly account for his height, the breadth of his shoulders, and the fact that despite his dark hair, did not look as conventionally French as she had expected.

58

"Your French is certainly exceptional," the *Duc* went on, "and I am not certain I am prepared to compare my English with it."

"If we are obliged to speak English, *Monsieur*," Canéda replied, "Ariel shall be the judge of how intelligible you are."

She spoke so provocatively and with such a look of mischief in her eyes, that the *Duc* made a little sound that might almost have been termed a laugh.

She was quite sure he did not laugh often, and she felt that, if nothing else, this was a point in her favour.

Then she saw Ben come through the gate and ride towards her, and she knew that the officers in the School watched him, and that his theatrical appearance undoubtedly amused them.

He looked very small on Black Boy's back. At the same time, he rode conventionally until he was half-way between the gates and the *Duc*.

Then he stood up in the saddle, holding only onto the reins while Black Boy carried him until they reached Canéda and were facing the *Duc*.

As the horse came to a standstill Ben swept off his top-hat and made a deep bow, then sat down in the saddle again.

The *Duc* however was looking at Black Boy rather than Ben and Canéda was sure it was deliberate.

"A fine animal," he said at length. "Can he do the same tricks as yours?"

"He is young and still a learner, as I wish to be, *Monsieur le Duc*."

"It is doubtful if there is much we can teach you," the *Duc* replied, "and as you have already given such an instructive performance, perhaps it would be unfair to ask for an encore."

Canéda gave him a dazzling smile.

"It would be a pleasure, *Monsieur,* if that is what you want."

"I feel that my officers would be very disappointed if, having aroused their interest and curiosity with an *aperitif* you denied them the rest of the meal."

Canéda gave a laugh that seemed to ring out infectiously.

"We will give a performance, *Monsieur,* but I warn you, I shall expect payment in kind."

"Of course, *mademoiselle,*" the *Duc* agreed.

Again he summoned an officer to his side and as he saluted respectfully Canéda was aware that the young man was looking at her rather than at the *Duc.*

"*Mademoiselle* Canéda has most graciously said she will show us what her horse can do, and I have promised in return, we will show her what we have achieved after two months of hard training."

There was a bite in the last words as if the *Duc* challenged the Cavalrymen not to let him down, and Canéda was sure he was a stern taskmaster and that the young officers would be afraid of him.

She was, however, concerned at the moment with looking at the jumps which were arranged in a circle round the centre of the ground on which they were standing.

They were almost as high as the wall which Ariel had just cleared, and arranged in a manner which made it sometimes difficult for a horse to take the second jump as easily as he took the first.

There was also an imitation wall made of loose bricks which it would be easy to dislodge at a touch.

Canéda glanced at Ben and she knew he was thinking there was nothing that need make Ariel or Black Boy the least apprehensive.

The ground was cleared and the Cavalrymen arranged themselves on either side.

She smiled at the *Duc.*

"I hope, *Monsieur,* that you will not be disappointed."

"I am quite certain, *Mademoiselle,* that would be impossible," the *Duc* replied.

His voice held a slightly dry note which did not make his words sound like a compliment, and Canéda told herself she would have to fight to get what she wanted, which in a way made it even more exhilarating.

She had only to look at the young officers watching her to know that she would see the admiration in their eyes which could so easily be heightened by a glance or a provocative little twist of her lips.

But with the *Duc* she was not certain.

She had surprised him. He had so far fallen in with her plans, but it might be difficult to extract any more.

However, for the moment she was only concerned to give a performance which would make him admire her horses if not herself.

There was no need for her to touch Ariel with her whip. She only had to speak to him in a voice he had always obeyed.

Then he was off, sailing over the jumps disdainfully, and treating the wall with contempt.

They went round twice then Canéda drew him up in the centre while Ben rode off on Black Boy.

Black Boy was a good jumper, but there was nothing particularly original about that.

It was Ben whom they watched.

He did the Cossack trick of travelling between the jumps at the side of his horse rather than in the saddle.

He stood up as he had when he arrived, but this time without holding onto the reins, and he vaulted to the ground and back onto Black Boy without making him slow his pace.

In fact, he did a dozen tricks that he had done in the Circus, but Canéda knew it was all the more remarkable because he had only been training Black Boy for the last nine months.

When finally he finished the course and trotted away there was a grin on his face that told her he was as pleased as she was that it had gone so well.

Then Canéda made Ariel dance again. He waltzed and polkaed as Juno used to do, and because there was no Band, Canéda hummed to him.

There were many other small tricks he could do which Canéda knew would impress the *Duc,* as only a really good horseman would know how difficult they were to teach, and the patience that was required to bring them to the perfection that Ariel showed.

Finally both Ariel and Black Boy went down on their knees and put their heads down on the ground, with their riders still sitting in the saddle.

It was then the applause broke out, and this time was accompanied by cheers and "Bravos" that seemed to echo round the Riding-School.

As the horses rose to their feet the *Duc* rode up to them.

"Thank you, *Mademoiselle*!" he said. "There is no need for me to tell you how magnificent your performance was, or how much it has been appreciated by me and the Officers of the Cavalry Corps."

Canéda bowed, and he continued:

"You have offered us a challenge, and now if you will stand at the saluting-base, we will see what we can offer you."

Canéda smiled at him, and they rode side by side to the saluting-base while Ben followed to stand behind them.

As if she had inspired the Cavalry Officers, they took their horses over the jumps in record time, first one man completing the course, then two together, and finally three.

It was impressive, and Canéda clapped her hands.

"You have trained them well, *Monsieur*."

"I am glad you did not visit us two months earlier, *Mademoiselle*," the *Duc* replied dryly.

Then the riders not only completed the course as quickly as they could, but dismounted, changed horses and went round again.

The best rider was incredibly quick, and Canéda decided this was certainly something she would try with Harry and his friends at Langstone Park.

She thought it would be a change from steeple-chasing, and was deciding what prize they would offer the winner when the *Duc* interrupted her thought.

The race had just finished and he said:

"I would now like to show you, *Mademoiselle*, what the horse I am riding can do. He is one of the best in my stable, and while he has no tricks to compare with Ariel's, I think you will agree that he is an excellent jumper."

He did not wait for Canéda answer, but started off over the jumps, and there was no doubt the horse he was riding was very superior to those they had watched before.

He could easily have jumped fences several feet higher than those that were erected in the School, and he had a style that Canéda recognised as being exceptional.

When the *Duc* came back to her she said enthusiastically:

"That was wonderful, *Monsieur*, really wonderful! I would love to ride such a remarkable animal, and feel as if I could jump over the moon!"

There was a little pause while she knew the *Duc* turned the idea over in his mind. Then he said:

"I should be delighted, *Mademoiselle*, for you to do so, but I think as it is now time for luncheon, wc should allow the horses to take a well-earned rest before the afternoon's programme."

Then he added:

"I should be honoured if you would give me the pleasure of having luncheon with me."

"I should be delighted, *Monsieur*, to accept your invitation," Canéda replied.

She felt a sudden surge of excitement, knowing her hopes had materialised, and her plan was working out. Whatever happened now, she had at least not failed ignominiously at the outset.

Then Canéda was riding beside the *Duc* with Ben following, out of the Riding-School through several narrow streets, before they reached the steep incline that led up the hill towards the Château.

The hill was steeper than Canéda looking up at it from below, had expected, and as they reached the top she saw the moat which surrounded the Castle.

There was the bridge over it which had once been a drawbridge in time of siege, but which now led them into a large courtyard in the centre of the Château.

Grooms came to take their horses and to look after Ben, while the *Duc* led Canéda through a great doorway, embellished with the Saumac coat-of-arms in stone. They climbed a stone staircase up to a large Salon with high, narrow windows looking out over the Loire valley.

Without speaking Canéda moved towards the nearest one and saw as she expected a view that was so breathtaking that she was, for the moment, speechless.

The Loire valley lay in front of her, the river winding through the flat green fields which swept away towards the misty horizon with many spires and castellated roofs peeping above the tops of the trees.

It was so lovely in the golden sunshine that she exclaimed:

"Now I feel as I have always wanted to do, that I am standing on 'the corner of the moon'!"

The *Duc* smiled.

"Shakespeare!" he said, "and – I think – Macbeth!"

"You are well read, *Monsieur*."

"I like to think so," he replied, "but I did not expect..."

He stopped and Canéda realised that he was suddenly aware of what he had been about to say and that it would have been rude to suggest that a woman from the Circus, whether she was English or French, would not have read Shakespeare.

She made no comment and he quickly pointed out the

roofs of a Château in the distance.

"I expect you would like to wash before we eat," he suggested, "and take off your hat. I would like to see your hair."

His tone was different from the way he had spoken before, and for a moment Canéda was surprised.

Then she remembered she was not a Lady who would resent such familiarity, but a Circus performer, and doubtless in the *Duc's* estimation a woman who was not particularly concerned over her morality or anybody else's.

With an effort she swept the surprise from her eyes and replied:

"Thank you. I am flattered, *Monsieur*."

Outside the Salon a maid-servant was waiting to take her to a large, beautifully furnished bedroom on the same floor.

It was so impressive and so exquisitely decorated that Canéda guessed it was one of the State-Rooms and wondered if it had been used by the famous *Duchesses* de Saumac.

She wanted to ask the maid if her supposition was correct, then thought it would be a mistake.

At the same time she was exceedingly intrigued that the *Duc's* mother had been English.

She wondered whether *Madame* de Goucourt had known this, but she supposed because the *Duchesse* had been ill for years she had not become well known in the Social World of the time.

Then there was the *Duc's* wife.

Had he loved her? Had he found her attractive, Canéda wondered, before she went mad?

Perhaps she had slept in this room and looking out of the window had not found the panoramic view attractive or felt as if she stood upon a corner of the moon, but instead had felt she was in a prison, cut off from all human contact with those far away below her.

As she washed her hands and took off her elegant riding-hat to tidy her hair, Canéda felt her imagination was running away with her, as her Nanny would have said.

This was all so exciting, and yet in a way frightening, because she was doing what she had no right to do and Harry would have considered it reprehensible.

She had never had luncheon or dined alone with a man before as she had always been strictly chaperoned since she arrived in London by one of the Lang aunts and she thought that, if nothing else, this would be an experience in itself.

Then she remembered she had a serious task ahead of her, and that was to intrigue, captivate and fascinate the *Duc*.

She looked at her reflection in the mirror.

Canéda would have been very foolish if she had not been aware that she was very lovely, with her straight, classical features.

Her sparkling blue eyes and a mischievous twist to her red lips constituted a snare for any man, unless he had locked away his heart behind steel doors, where no-one could reach it.

"Is that what happened to the *Duc* after his wife went mad?" Canéda asked.

Had he in consequence almost a dislike of women? She was somehow sure that was not true.

There was something about him, autocratic though he might seem, which told her he was very masculine!

There was a smile on Canéda's lips as, having thanked the maid-servant, she walked back towards the Salon.

She knew her riding-habit did not make her look out of place, because it was of silk and was fashioned more like a gown than a habit.

It fastened down the back, and had a collar that was low round her neck with a soft bow in the front above the large pearl buttons and white braid.

The *Duc* was waiting for her, standing in front of a large

mediaeval fireplace.

He did not move as she entered the Salon, but watched her walk towards him in the same way, Canéda thought, as he had watched the horses take their fences.

As he did so, she had the feeling that he was trying to be critical and although she thought it was an impertinence, it was still a move in the right direction.

He waited until she was beside him before he said:

"You walk with a grace that is surprising."

"Why surprising?" Canéda enquired.

"Because most women who ride as well as you do not dance as well as they sit a horse, but I would not mind waging a large sum that you are a remarkable dancer."

"I think I should allow you to judge that for yourself," Canéda answered.

"But of course, that is what I am hoping you will do," the *Duc* replied.

A servant approached with glasses of wine.

"This is from my own vineyards, and I hope it will please you," the *Duc* said.

The wine was cool and delicious, and because instantly her mind went to the vineyards belonging to her grand-parents Canéda said:

"The vines here are in good heart?"

"I have no complaints," the *Duc* replied.

"I had heard, and it must have been from someone in Angers, that there is an outbreak of phylloxera in the Dordogne region."

"It is very serious," the *Duc* said quietly, "and we can only pray that in the North we shall remain immune."

Canéda did not pursue the subject – she had found out what she wanted to know.

Then as they went into luncheon in a room almost as large as the Salon and again with long narrow windows looking both North and East, she set herself out to amuse the *Duc*.

She told him of the race-meetings she had been to in

England, of the horses that were for sale in Tattersall's Sale Rooms, of the successes on the turf gained by members of the Jockey Club.

She drew freely on her imagination and also remembered many amusing things that Harry had told her of the race-meetings which she had not attended personally, but at which he had been present.

The *Duc* laughed several times and a sideways glance she noticed from one of the flunkeys, told her it was a sound they did not ofter hear in the Château.

Finally when after a delectable meal, the coffee had been poured out and Canéda at the *Duc's* insistence had accepted a small glass of liqueur made from strawberries, the servants withdrew and she said:

"Now it is only fair for you to tell me about yourself."

"What do you want to know about me?" he parried, "and what induced you to come here, and indeed approach me in such an unusual manner?"

"It is quite simple, Canéda replied, "I wanted to see your Riding-School, and I was quite certain you would have a notice on the gate saying: 'Women Keep Out!' "

The *Duc* smiled.

"But you entered in a somewhat unconventional manner. I suppose you realise it was a dangerous thing to do?"

"Why? Ariel made light of it."

"You might not have landed on the sand, and there might have been something in the way. It is a risk you must never take again."

"It is a risk I have no wish to take, if the gate is open to me."

"There is no need for me to tell you that you may ride in the School whenever you wish, but not during the hours when the Officers are having their lessons."

Canéda raised her eye-brows, and he said:

"You must be well aware, *Mademoiselle*, that you would be, to put it mildly, a distraction."

Canéda gave a little laugh.

"I am not certain whether you are flattering me, or insulting me, *Monsieur*, but let me promise you I will not interfere with your lessons for long. I am only passing through this part of the country."

"To where?"

She made a vague little gesture with her hands.

"I am not quite certain. Shall I say I am exploring France?"

"You sound as if this is the first time you have been here."

"It is!"

"And yet your mother was French?"

"We lived in England, and she was very poor."

This was at least the truth, and Canéda was determined to lie as little as possible, which was why she had not given herself a false name.

She remembered her father saying to her a long time ago.

"If one is going to lie, one should tell a really good one, and as near the truth as possible."

Her mother had given a cry of protest.

"Really, Gerald, how can you say such things to the child? You know as well as I do she should not lie in any circumstances."

"You cannot go through life always telling the truth on every occasion," Canéda's father had replied. "Nothing is more uncomfortable or disagreeable than someone who tells the truth for what he calls, your own good."

"You know that is not what I am talking about," Mrs. Lang had said. "I loathe lies of all sorts, and I want Canéda to tell the truth and take the consequences."

"You are so good, and I love you for it, my darling, but I think Canéda will find in life that it is sometimes easier to 'trim one's sails to the wind'."

"You are not to listen, Canéda," her mother admonished her.

At the same time she had smiled as she spoke and it was

not really a rebuke.

Canéda in fact, hated lies as her mother' hated them, and only when it would be unkind or rude to be too frank did she 'trim her sails to the wind'.

Now she decided she would be as truthful as possible while masquerading as somebody very different from herself.

She took a sip of her liqueur and realised the *Duc* was watching her.

There was still not the glint of admiration she had hoped for in his eyes, but at least she held his attention, and she was almost sure that she intrigued him and he wanted to know more about her.

"Who is travelling with you on this trip?" he asked.

"I am with a friend."

She spoke lightly before she realised what he might infer from the remark.

"I am sure he is very charming," he said with a twist of his lips.

"As it happens, it is not a man, but a woman. A Frenchwoman, who was anxious to return to the country from which she came to see her relatives and friends, and so we came together."

"And she is with you now?"

"She is not far from here."

There was a little pause. Then the *Duc* said:

"Supposing I invite you to stay with me while you learn what you wish to learn from my horses? Would I have to extend the invitation to her as well?"

Canéda shook her head.

"No. In fact, I am quite certain she would rather be with the people she loves."

"And whom do you love?" the *Duc* enquired.

Canéda was astonished at the question and for a moment she felt she could not have heard him aright.

Then she told herself once again that if he was over-familiar it was because of the way she was dressed.

"Why should you suspect that I love anybody?" she asked.

"I cannot believe," he replied, "that your horse, magnificent though he is, fills your life to the exclusion of everybody else, and I suppose even Englishmen have eyes in their heads!"

"They have!" Canéda agreed, "but for the moment I am curious about Frenchmen. You see, *Monsieur,* they are not a species one meets very often in England, not in the places where I have been."

That again was true, Canéda thought. There were no Frenchmen living within fifty miles of the village and the only ones she knew were those who visited her father and mother when they came over from France.

But the visitors were mostly women like *Madame* de Goucourt, whose husband was too occupied and too busy to come to the country.

"There are plenty of Frenchmen at the Riding-School," the *Duc* replied, "and they are, as you have seen, only too eager to make your acquaintance."

"For the moment I am content to talk to you," Canéda said. "Do you live here in this enormous Château all by yourself?"

"I am not always alone – but most of the time."

"What do you do...read?"

"A great deal."

"But you must feel lonely."

"There is plenty of companionship if I need it."

"Do you mean the Officers in the School? You see them in the daytime."

There was a smile on his lips as if he was aware what Canéda was trying to find out, and he said:

"I am alone only if I wish to be."

The way he looked was more eloquent than words, and it suddenly struck Canéda that of course, he had a mistress.

The books she had read had told her that Frenchmen

were ardent lovers and that Kings like François I had wandered around the town at night incognito in search of attractive women.

And of course, Louise the XIV and Louis XV had had innumerable mistresses. She had read about *Madame* de Pompadour and *Madame* de Maintenon, and all the others.

But it had never crossed her mind that while the *Duc's* wife was locked away because she was mad, that would not preclude him from enjoying female companionship.

Perhaps some of her thoughts revealed themselves in her eyes for the *Duc* asked mockingly:

"Surely you did not expect anything else?"

"I was just being…curious about you…living here on the…corner of the moon, apparently…alone."

She did not know why, but it was disconcerting to find the *Duc* had women to amuse him.

She had somehow expected, from what had been said about him, that he was a monogamist, and because fate had destroyed his married life, he would no longer be concerned with the female sex.

"Even the moon has adjacent stars twinkling around it," he said.

Of course, Canéda told herself, there would be women in his life.

He was far too attractive as a man, and of course as a *Duc* and a rich one, women would flock to him like bees round a honey-pot.

"Of course," she agreed aloud, and thought her voice sounded a little bleak.

For the first time things did not seem to be going so smoothly.

She had somehow expected to walk in, beautiful, sensational, and take him by storm because he was cynical and embittered by the way he had been treated by fate.

It was disconcerting to find that he was obviously well content with his life as it was and was missing none of the comforts that only a woman could give him.

Canéda put down her glass.

"Perhaps we should get back to the Riding-School."

"There is no hurry," the *Duc* replied. "Come and sit in a room where I think we will be more comfortable."

He rose as he spoke and when they left the Dining-Room they did not return to the Salon where they had been earlier.

Instead the *Duc* took her along a passage and opened the door which led into one of the most intriguing rooms she had ever seen.

It was small and round, and she knew that it must be situated in one of the towers which stood at each of the four corners of the Château.

There were windows looking in three directions and a large, comfortable sofa covered with silk cushions which the *Duc* indicated as a place for Canéda to sit.

Instead she stood at the window looking out once again on the amazing panorama and the silver river that seemed to grow longer and go further every time she looked at it.

She stood there for sometime, aware without turning her head that the *Duc* was watching her.

"Well?" he asked at length. "Are you still content with the moon, or do you wish to come back to the earth with all its troubles?"

"I have none at the moment."

"Then you are very lucky!"

"What are yours?"

She turned from the window as she asked the question to face him.

"I have none except the difficulty of deciding whether you are real or just a figment of my imagination."

"I assure you I am very real."

"And very different from anyone I have ever seen before," the *Duc* finished. "I may be wrong, but I have a feeling that how you appear on the surface may not be quite genuine."

Canéda started.

"Why should you think that?" she asked quickly.

"Shall I say that living up here on what you call the moon, I have grown perceptive about people. I use my instinct rather than my ears."

Without really thinking, because they had been speaking of Shakespeare, Canéda quoted:

" *'Love looks not with the eyes, but with the mind.'* "

Even as she said the words she blushed knowing it was a mistake to mention love, but it was too late to retract.

"Now the most abused word in the French language appears," the *Duc* remarked. "*L'amour*! I wondered when we would get around to it."

"That is not what I meant, as you are well aware, *Monsieur*," Canéda said almost crossly. "I was merely quoting from *A Midsummer Night's Dream.* "

"I know that," the *Duc* said, "and I thought perhaps I should have quoted that particular play when you talked about my being alone. Surely you remember – *'One grows, lives and dies in single blessedness?'* "

Canéda thought he was throwing her a challenge, but because she could not say that his single blessedness was thrust upon him because of his wife's madness, and feeling the whole conversation was becoming somewhat uncomfortable, she moved from the window to sit down on the sofa.

"I must go now," she said in a different tone of voice. "Ben and I have quite a long ride to get back to where we are staying."

"I have already suggested that you might prefer to stay with me," the *Duc* said.

The question "unchaperoned?" trembled on Canéda's lips. Then she told herself he would think her idiotic if she said anything so superfluous.

Of course a woman from the Circus would not expect to be chaperoned.

Then while she thought it would be amusing and a step

74

forward to stay with the *Duc,* she wondered what else he might expect if she did so.

Then she told herself she was sure that she could look after herself.

She knew that for her to stay at the Château without *Madame* de Goucourt would make Harry very angry, and certainly it was something of which her mother would not have approved.

But she had wanted the *Duc* to invite her and now he had done so, and it seemed foolish to back off from the very moment when she could give him a short, sharp lesson and leave him, she hoped, disconsolate without her.

'If I can only see him in the daytime, it will take much longer to get him in the position in which I want him,' Canéda thought to herself, 'which is at my feet, where Lord Warrington and all those other men have been.'

It was as if her thoughts had been discernible in her eyes, because after a moment the *Duc* said:

"I am not in the habit of having my invitations considered so carefully."

"I am trying to make up my mind whether to say 'yes,' or 'no'."

"That is obvious!" the *Duc* replied. "Most people to whom I extend my hospitality are only too eager to accept it."

"I am glad if I am different," Canéda retorted.

"I shall be very disappointed if you are so different that you refuse me."

Canéda looked down aand her long eye-lashes were dark against her cheeks.

"What I am wondering, *Monsieur*, is what you…expect from your…guests when you…entertain them."

As if he understood what she was trying hesitatingly to say, the *Duc* smiled before he replied:

"Shall I answer that by saying as much as you are prepared to give? I am not an Ogre, or a Barbarian."

Canéda drew in her breath. Then she said:

"With that assurance, *Monsieur*, I am delighted to accept your invitation."

"Then what we will do," the *Duc* said, "is to send your man back to collect what clothes you need. He can take one of my carriages, and if he leaves soon he can be back in plenty of time for you to look beautiful at dinner."

"I will certainly try," Canéda replied, "but now I want to ride your horse, as you promised me I could."

The *Duc* opened the door and she went back to the bedroom to put on her riding-hat.

As she looked at herself in the mirror, she could not but feel a little tremor of fear when she thought how angry Harry would be if he had any idea what she was doing.

Then she told herself what the eye did not see the heart would not grieve over.

He need never know that she had done anything so outrageous, only that she had taken her revenge on the *Duc* as she had intended to do when she had left England.

There was still *Madame* de Goucourt to contend with and Canéda sat down at a *secretaire* in the corner of the bedroom and carefully choosing a plain piece of writing paper that was not embossed with the name of the Château, she wrote a quick note.

She told *Madame* that she had decided to stay the night with the friend she was visiting and hoped to be back tomorrow.

She finished:

> *Do not Worry about me, Dear*
> Madame, *I am well looked after,*
> *and I will return tomorrow. Enjoy*
> *yourself with Your friends, and We*
> *will compare Notes later.*
> *My love and Gratitude,*
> *Yours affectionately,*
> *Canéda.*

She sealed the letter, addressed it to *Madame* de Gourcourt, and put it in her pocket so that she could give it to Ben without the *Duc* seeing it.

'I am behaving very badly,' she thought as she left the bedroom knowing she would return to it later.

Then she thought that at least it was fun, but perhaps that was an inadequate word.

It was intriguing and exciting and splendidly exhilarating to think that her revenge on the *Duc* de Saumac was working out exactly in the way she had intended.

CHAPTER FOUR

Riding around the School on the *Duc's* grey horse, Canéda thought she had never enjoyed herself more.

Although she had ridden constantly with Harry and they had raced against each other, she had been aware, because he was older than she was and a more experienced rider, he would always be the winner.

But she had with Ariel just beaten all the Officers competing against her over a timed course, and now she was attempting to beat the *Duc*.

He had challenged her, saying:

"Up to now I have been the judge. Now I think I should be a participator."

Because she thought it might annoy him and also draw his attention, she had replied:

"But of course, and I would be prepared, if you are faster than I am, to concede victory on one condition."

"What is that?" he enquired.

"That you allow me to ride *Toujours*."

This was the name, she had discovered, of his grey horse, and she had the feeling that he was very confident of winning because *Toujours* was, in his way, as exceptional as Ariel.

The *Duc* hesitated before he replied and she saw the twinkle in his eyes.

"Are you suggesting," he asked, "that I should have an unfair advantage if I rode my own horse?"

"But of course you would!" Cané replied. "*Toujours* knows the course far better than Ariel, and I am sure that the reason you have not competed before was that you felt it unsporting not to give your competitors a chance."

The *Duc* laughed.

"Very well," he said. "You shall ride *Toujours* and I will choose another mount."

He gave an order to one of the grooms who brought forward a horse that had not jumped so far.

He was a young chestnut and only to look at him made Canéda aware that he would be very fast.

She was, however, delighted to think that she could ride the *Duc's* horse, because she knew from the expression on the faces of his Officers that never before had anyone been allowed to mount him except his owner.

Because she was very experienced in handling horses and both Harry and Ben had taught her how to control them, she did not attempt to mount *Toujours* until she had made a great fuss of him.

She patted his neck, stroked his nose and talked to him in a soft, beguiling voice and only when she felt the horse was really aware of her did she move to his side to show she was ready to be helped into the saddle.

The groom would have done so, but the *Duc* gestured him to one side.

Instead of cupping his hands in the usual way he stretched out his fingers on each side of her tiny waist and lifted her into the air.

For one moment as he did so their faces were very close together and she thought there was the expression in his grey eyes that she had hoped to see.

The she was seated in the saddle and the *Duc* with an experienced hand arranged her skirt over her stirrup.

She moved *Toujours* into position, then waited while the *Duc* took out his stop-watch.

"*Bonne chance!*" all the young Officers were murmuring.

The *Duc* was very businesslike as he asked:

"Are you ready, *Mademoiselle*?"

"I am ready, *Monsieur.*"

"Then – Go!"

He pressed the button of the stop-watch and there was no need for Canéda to use either her whip or spur on *Toujours*.

He knew exactly what was expected of him and he took the first fence magnificently.

He was a very large horse, higher even than Ariel, and she found it a thrilling experience to ride something so magnificent and as a special privilege accorded only to her.

They went round the course in what she was sure was record time, and there were cheers and applause from the Officers who were watching.

Then as she drew *Toujours* to a standstill in front of the *Duc,* they rushd forward exclaiming:

"Magnificent! Fantastic! You were sensational, *Mademoiselle!*"

"I had a sensational horse," Canéda replied.

She would have slipped from the saddle, but before she could do so the *Duc* was there to lift her to the ground.

As he did so, she said:

"I admit, *Monsieur,* that *Toujours* is the second most wonderful horse in the world!"

"Both he and I are honoured!" the *Duc* replied formally.

She thought, although she was not sure, that he lifted her down more slowly than he need have done and that his hands lingered for a moment on her waist.

Then he turned to mount the chestnut and a Senior Officer had the stop-watch in his hand.

Watching him Canéda knew that he rode better than any man she had ever seen in her life.

She had felt that no-one could be a better rider than her father until Harry grew up.

Now, although she hated to admit it, the *Duc* was better than either of them.

There was something about the way he rode that made

him seem a part of his horse, in that they moved in unison and with a rhythm that was almost like hearing the sound of music.

He did not appear to hurry, but she knew as he reached the last two fences that the Officers were tense and she herself held her breath.

One second – two seconds.

He brought the chestnut to a standstill and the Officer holding the stop-watch said:

"You are the winner, *Monsieur le Duc,* by half a second!"

A cheer went up but it was somewhat half-hearted after the applause Canéda had received.

The *Duc* dismounted and walked to her side.

"Are you satisfied?" he asked.

She raised her eye-brows at the strange question.

"That I was not cheating," he explained.

"I did not think you would do so, and anyway I was only teasing. Moreover, though it may surprise you, I am aware that as a woman I am expected to take second place."

"Most women expect to be first in everything," the *Duc* answered.

"Except of course in sport."

She saw by his smile that her reply amused him.

When they returned to the Château they duelled with each other in words, and again Canéda found it an amusing experience that she had not known before.

She had always been aware that she had a quick brain and would like to argue and exchange views with a man.

But the men ever since she had been in London had persisted in flattering her, to the exclusion of all other conversation.

Whatever she tried to talk about, the subject always got back to love in one way or another, but now with the *Duc* every word they spoke was more like a rapier thrust.

She had the feeling while she was sparring with him that

he was determined to be the victor not only in riding, but also because he was a man and she was a woman.

He was so essentially masculine that she found herself vividly conscious of him even when he was silent.

She was sure he would be very difficult to understand and she realised how easy it had been for him to build up a reputation of being awe-inspiring and aloof from other people.

The mere fact that he lived alone in his fantastic fortress of a Château far above the earth below him and was not interested in the Social life that was so much a part of the Loire valley, made him a law unto himself.

When they arrived back at the Château Canéda found that Ben had not yet returned with her clothes.

She therefore merely took off her hat as she had for luncheon, and having washed, joined the *Duc* in the tower Sitting-Room where he told her he would be waiting for her.

To her surprise, there was beside the sofa a small table and on a silver tray there was what was obviously an English silver tea-pot and a number of patisseries.

Canéda gave a little laugh of delight.

"You are very considerate, *Monsieur*."

"I know the English are at a loss without their cups of tea."

"I am astonished that you should be aware of that," Canéda said remembering that his mother had died when he was very young.

"Shall I say that I have been taught a number of English customs by one of your countrywomen?"

Canéda knew by the way he spoke that she had been someone close to him, and she did not know why, but she felt a little tug of her heart.

She sat down on the sofa and poured herself out a cup of tea saying:

"I presume, as you are being very French at the moment, you do not wish to join me."

He was obviously more perceptive even than she had suspected, for he replied:

"Because I suggested I have a *Chère Amie?* What else do you expect?"

"I expect nothing, *Monsieur.* Why should I?"

"Because like all women," he said cynically, "you like to think of a man with a wife constantly at his side."

"I think you are putting words into my mouth," Canéda said sharply.

"But it is true," he persisted. "I can assure you that I am very happy living in my corner of the moon, although of course, you will understand I occasionally step down from the sky and mix with mere mortals on the earth below."

Canéda knew that he was mocking her, and she resented it because he was making her feel as if she had been rather gauche and foolish.

She set the tea-pot down, and said:

"Perhaps I have interrupted your plans and engagements, and the best thing I could do would be to return to my friend."

The *Duc* laughed.

"Now you are definitely trying to punish me for a crime I have not committed, and I reiterate, you are interrupting nothing. If you were not here I should have dined alone in all my glory!"

"And that would have amused you?"

"The answer actually is 'yes', the *Duc* replied. "I have learned to be self-sufficient, and when I am alone I have books and a certain amount of work to do."

"What sort of work?"

"I keep a record of the horses who pass through my School and the men who ride them. I am also compiling a Thesis on the schooling of horses."

"That is wonderful!" Canéda exclaimed. "Please may I have a copy of it?"

"It is not yet finished," the *Duc* replied, "but of course I will send you one if you will give me an address."

"That might be difficult, as I am a wanderer on the face of the earth! It is only by chance that I have dropped in on the moon in passing."

He gave her a shrewd glance which told her that he was not deceived by this remark.

"By chance?" he questioned. "I doubt that!"

"Why should you do so?"

"Because your entrance was too well thought out. You must have known that I would be in the School at that particular time, and you must also have known, because you care for your horse, where it was safe to jump the wall."

He was more intuitive than she had expected he would be, and because she did not wish to be drawn into a discussion as to why she was there, Canéda relapsed into silence.

He sat looking at her until he said:

"Tell me about the Circus to which you belong, if in fact, it exists."

"Why should you doubt that it does?"

"Because I find it hard to believe, despite your expertise on Ariel that you perform in a Circus, or that you have ever mixed with the type of person one finds in them."

"What do you know about Circuses?"

"Quite a lot, as it happens," the *Duc* replied. "A number of them come here every summer because they hope to sell me their horses. It may surprise you, but the chestnut on which I beat you this afternoon was born in a Circus."

"Like Ariel!" Canéda exclaimed.

Then because she wanted to convince him that she was with a Circus she told him about Juno and her death, and how all she had left behind was Ariel and Ben.

She saw the *Duc* was interested, and when she had finished he said:

"You are too young and too lovely for such a life

Surely there is something else you could do like – getting married?"

"To one of the clowns?" Canéda asked lightly.

"If marriage is not on your programme," the *Duc* said, "I can only imagine you have a rich Protector."

He spoke quite casually, but the colour flared into Canéda's cheeks as she said sharply:

"How dare you suggest such a thing! And you are quite wrong."

She was so positive that the *Duc* said:

"I must apologise if I have insulted you, but I cannot believe a Circus proprietor, unless he is a very exceptional one, would have provided you with the habit you are wearing now, and which undoubtedly cost at least double the salary an ordinary Circus performer could earn in six months."

Canéda was so surprised that she forgot to be angry and stared at him wide-eyed.

"How can you know something like that?"

The *Duc's* lips twisted and there was no need for explanation.

Because she felt she was fighting a losing battle Canéda rose from the sofa to walk to the window and look out again at the view.

The sun was beginning to sink on the horizon, and the sky above it was a blaze of colour.

She was so absorbed in its beauty that she started when the *Duc* spoke just behind her because she was not aware that he had risen from his chair.

"Are you still considering whether or not to leave me?" he asked. "I shall almost certainly prevent you from doing so."

"How would you do that?" Canéda enquired.

"I suppose I could always lock you in the dungeons which are below the level of the moat and very unpleasant," the *Duc* replied, "but instead I will merely plead with you to keep me company as I want you to."

There was a note now in his voice which Canéda knew she had been waiting to hear, and yet somehow it did not give her the elation she had hoped for. Instead it seemed in some way to vibrate within her and evoke a response she had not expected.

"I still...think I would be...wise to...go."

"Because I have shocked you?"

She raised her chin.

"I did not say you have...done that."

"Nevertheless, I think it is what has happened," the *Duc* said.

He drew nearer and stood beside her at the window where he could look at her profile against the grey stone.

She did not move but kept her eyes on the sunset, and after what seemed a long time, he said:

"You are very beautiful and, as dozens of men must have told you, your blue eyes fringed with dark lashes are enchantingly original."

He spoke in the dry way that was habitual to him, and he did not make it sound such a compliment as it would have been from any other man.

Because she was afraid that the conversation had grown too serious and too personal Canéda said:

"My eyes are English, but my lashes and my hair are French. You can make a choice of which you prefer."

"As a Frenchman I am for the moment intrigued by the English," the *Duc* replied, "so shall we speak that language for a change?"

The last sentence was spoken in English, and Canéda gave a little cry as she exclaimed:

"But that is good!"

"I had an English mother, an English Nanny, and at one time an English Governess," the *Duc* explained.

"They certainly did a good job!"

It was true. The *Duc* had only the very faintest shadow of an accent, but because he was speaking English she felt, although it was ridiculous, that he was not quite so menacing as he had been when he spoke in French.

She gave him a mischievous glance as she said:

"Now you are speaking like an Englishman you must behave like one, and we must start talking about horses instead of ourselves."

"Quite frankly, I only want to talk about you," the *Duc* said. "You intrigue me and, shall I add, I am very curious."

It was exactly what she had wanted him to be, Canéda thought, and she told herself she had been very clever.

She turned her face once again to the window.

"I think it would be a mistake to be too prosaic about detail," she said. "You admit this is an enchanted place outside the ordinary mundane world of human beings. Very well, for the moment we are not human."

"Then what are we?"

Canéda gave him an enchanting smile.

"You, of course, are the Man in the Moon and I am just a shooting star who has called in."

"A very good description!" the *Duc* approved. "You shine like a star, and you certainly dress like one."

His eyes flickered for a moment over her pink riding-habit and Canéda was suddenly aware that because she had intended to look theatrical her bodice was very tight and revealed the curves of her breasts.

Her waist was accentuated more than she would have considered proper in one of her ordinary habits.

She felt shy and wished that she had relied on her riding to attract his attention rather than on the theatrical effect of her clothes and those in which she had dressed Ben.

Because she was afraid of what the *Duc* was thinking, she said quickly:

"I am sure Ben will be back by now with my luggage, and if possible I would like a bath before dinner."

"Of course," the *Duc* replied. "I am sure that has been arranged and as I have a great deal to talk to you about shall we dine early?"

He took his watch from his waist-coat pocket and said:

"I will meet you here in an hour."

"An hour will suit me perfectly," Canéda replied, "and thank you, *Monsieur*, for a very entertaining afternoon."

She would have passed him to leave the room, but he reached out, took her hand in his and raised it to his lips.

"I must thank you," he said, "for an experience I shall not forget."

She felt his lips on her skin and it gave her a strange sensation.

Many men had kissed her hand, but somehow this was different, and she did not wish to think why.

Instead she moved quickly away from him, and he only just had time to open the door for her.

As she hurried along the passage to go to her bedroom she had the feeling that she was escaping from something that was frightening, yet exciting, and at the same time menacing.

She opened the door of her bedroom and found the maid was unpacking the things she had listed for Ben to bring back from the Inn.

He could have taken one of the *Duc's* chaises, but because Canéda was very anxious that no-one at the Château should know where she was staying, she had insisted that Ben went on horse-back.

"Can you manage everything I will want? she had asked.

"Yes, I can, M'Lady," Ben replied.

"Remember it is very important that the servants should not know where I am staying."

"Ye can trust I, M'Lady."

Canéda had put the list into his hand.

"Remind my maid that the gown I require is the pink one that I told her to pack apart from the others."

"I'll remind her, M'Lady."

"If you see *Madame* de Goucourt, and I hope you will not," Canéda went on, "tell her I shall be back tomorrow, and that everything is all right."

"Leave it to I, M'Lady."

Canéda was just about to send him away when she had a sudden thought.

She went close to him and spoke in a very low voice, just in case they should be overheard.

She knew as he nodded agreement to everything she said that he would not fail her. Then as he hurried away she had gone back to where the *Duc* was waiting for her with a smile on her lips.

This had been after luncheon, and Ben had had plenty of time to reach the Inn and return.

She wished she could speak to him and find out if everything was all right, and *Madame* de Goucourt was not upset at the thought of her staying away.

Then Canéda told herself there was no reason to worry.

The maid in the bedroom was shaking out the gown that had been packed in such a way that it could be carried on the back of a saddle.

It was in pink, but Canéda saw that it was not the gown she had asked for.

When she had left England she had deliberately not taken with her the experienced, older lady's-maid who had been looking after her since Harry had inherited the title and they could afford the best servants.

She was a woman Canéda both liked and trusted but because she had always been in the 'best houses' she was not the type of maid she wanted on this particular journey.

She had therefore insisted on taking with her one of the young housemaids, an honest, hard-working girl who was obviously not over-blessed with brains.

Canéda knew she would do as she was told and not ask too many questions and that was what she required.

She said her own lady's-maid could have a holiday and she had also discovered fortunately that she hated the sea and was seasick at the sight of a wave.

She had therefore packed everything that Canéda needed, giving the younger maid innumerable instructions that she only half understood, and who was too excited at the prospect of going abroad to worry about anything else.

'It is typical of her stupidity,' Canéda thought, 'that while she has sent me a pink gown, it is not the flamboyant one I chose for this occasion.'

She had bought the pink gown at the same time as she had the pink riding-habit with which to attract the *Duc* and make him really believe that she was a performer in a Circus.

Instead what had arrived with Ben was a very expensive, very lovely gown from one of the most exclusive Bond Street dressmakers who prided herself on giving her clients Paris *chic*.

Looking at it as the French maid hung it up in the wardrobe, Canéda wondered what the *Duc* would think of it, and had the uncomfortable feeling it would make him more suspicious than he was already that she was not what she appeared to be.

Then she told herself it was immaterial what he did think.

She was certain he was already becoming enamoured of her and when she had made sure of it she could disappear as she wished to do, leaving him, she hoped, unhappy and frustrated.

It had seemed such a clever idea when she had planned it all in England and during the voyage, and yet now, even when it was working exactly as she had intended, she felt anxious.

In her imagination the *Duc* had only been a cardboard man without reality and not made of flesh and blood.

He had just been a boy in the story that had started when her mother had run away from his father and married the man to whom she had given her heart. As a result of which his father, the old *Duc* had sworn his revenge and tried to make life intolerable for his rival.

It was the sort of tale, Canéda often thought, that should have been written by a novelist.

And what could have been a better ending than that her father and mother had been so happy?

It was she who had refused to allow the tale to end there.

She had always wanted to avenge herself on the *Duc* who had hurt her father, and on her grandparents who had been so heartless towards her mother.

The opportunity had come with the arrival of her grandmother's letter, and now a new story was unfolding itself and she was actually here in the Ogre's Castle.

It only remained for her to carry out the rest of her plan and the first chapter in her pursuit of revenge would have ended.

Then on to the next.

As she bathed in water scented with a fragrance distilled from camellias Canéda continued to her surprise, to feel apprehensive.

Why she should do so she had no idea, and she told herself she was not really afraid of being alone in the Château with the *Duc*.

He might seem raffish but he was a gentleman, and she could not believe he would not respect her wishes or that she could not, as she had told herself at the beginning, look after herself.

She had always known it was only cads and bounders who forced themselves on women who did not want them.

All the men who had approached her, even though they were madly in love, had obeyed her when she had refused to let them kiss her, and although they had pleaded with her on many occasions not to leave them, they had not tried to prevent her from doing so.

The *Duc* would be the same, Canéda thought as she dried herself on a soft towel.

It struck her that perhaps, because she was pretending to be not a Lady but a Circus performer, his attitude might be different.

Then she reassured herself by thinking she was a woman, and as such able to command the respect of a man however lowly he might suppose her to be.

At the same time she found herself thinking that she ought not to have agreed to stay the night.

'Harry would be horrified!' she thought.

And she did not pretend that her father and mother would not have been shocked.

Then she put up her chin.

"The end justifies the means," she told herself.

She was quoting an old Jesuit adage, and the end she was aiming for was that the *Duc* should be humiliated in wanting a woman who eluded him and who had vanished from his life after he had expressed a desire for her to stay.

'Perhaps...he will...ask me to become his...mistress,' Canéda thought.

She could not help remembering that he had made it clear that he was not always alone, and she told herself that she had been very foolish.

Of course there would be women in his life and it was distinctly annoying that one of them had been English.

Canéda wondered what she had been like: fair and blue-eyed, she supposed, as a Frenchman would expect an Englishwoman to be, just as she had expected him to have dark eyes instead of grey ones.

She tried to reassure herself that if, as he said, he was half-English he would have an Englishman's code of honour where she was concerned.

He would therefore behave in the same way as Lord Warrington, or the other men who had asked her to marry them.

They had begged her and had even threatened to destroy themselves if she would not say 'yes'.

But they had never tried to molest her, kiss her against her will, or even touch her if she did not want them to.

"The *Duc* will be the same," Canéda decided as she

instructed the maid who was waiting on her how to arrange her hair.

When she was dressed she stared into the mirror and with a little frown realised she looked very different from what she had intended.

The gown she had asked for and her stupid maid had not sent was a bright shade of pink embroidered with sequins and diamanté, over-elaborate even though the fashion at the moment was for heavily decorated evening gowns.

As she was small Canéda had thought them too over-powering and had therefore chosen gowns that really had a French *chic* about them because they relied on line rather than decoration.

The one she was wearing now was soft, almond-blossom pink, and it was almost plain compared to the gowns worn by other débutantes.

Yet because it revealed Canéda's perfect figure and tiny waist it made her, with the front swept into a bustle at the back, look like a young goddess stepping out of the rising sun to bring life and beauty to a dark world.

Canéda had also bought before she left London some false theatrical jewellery that she intended to wear instead of her real jewels.

In her hurry she had said: "Just pack the necklace, bracelets and stars that go with the pink gown," and thought her maid would understand.

Instead she had packed Canéda's real jewellery and although she thought the *Duc* might look at them questioningly, she wanted to wear them because she knew they complemented the elegance of her gown.

There were three stars to arrange in her hair besides a small necklace of real pearls which Harry had given her, and a narrow bracelet of diamonds and pearls which they had found in the Langstone collection amongst other jewels which had belonged to the late Countess.

Some of them were magnificent and obviously were

family heirlooms.

Harry had put those in the safe saying that Canéda was too young for them, but of the rest he had said carelessly:

"Wear them until I want them for my wife, and you have a husband who will give you better ones."

Canéda had thanked him and because she liked jewellery but had never had any, she had worn the smaller brooches, necklaces and bracelets, and enjoyed doing so.

Now she thought as she looked at her reflection she looked much more like a débutante than a Circus performer and certainly and unmistakably a Lady.

Then she told herself there was nothing she could do about it except put a little extra lip-salve on her lips.

When she had done so, her mouth seemed in contrast to the rest of her appearance to create a jarring note, so she wiped the salve away and turned from the mirror.

She thanked the maid, then went from the bedroom and walked down the passage towards the room in the tower with a lilt in her step.

However reprehensible, however wrong what she was doing might be, it was still an adventure!

An adventure to be in this magnificent Château high above the world, and to dine alone with the most enigmatic and certainly the most interesting man she had ever met.

A servant opened the door and she entered to find the candles had been lit although there was still a faint light from the setting sun coming through the uncurtained windows.

The room held an atmosphere of mystery but it was impossible for the moment to think of anything but the *Duc*.

If he had seemed impressive in his plain, well-cut riding-clothes he looked very different in evening-dress. In fact, there was a magnificence about him and Canéda thought that if she had seen him anywhere in England he would still have been outstanding and it would have been impossible not to notice him.

She stood still for a moment, just inside the door looking at him as he stood with his back to the fireplace in which a fire had been lit. Their eyes met and it was impossible to look away.

Almost as if it was an effort she walked towards him and he said:

"That is how you always ought to look. I know now what was wrong."

"Wrong?" Canéda questioned, even though she knew exactly what he meant.

"The fancy dress," he said. "Effective, undoubtedly eye-catching, but let me add quite unnecessary."

Because it was what she thought herself, Canéda felt for a moment as if she had no answer ready and inexplicably, for it was something she never was, she felt shy.

The *Duc* took a glass of champagne that was waiting on a side table and put it into her hands.

"As this is our first dinner together," he said, "I feel I should drink a toast, but it is difficult to find the right words."

"Surely that is unusual for a Frenchman?" Canéda managed to reply.

"I think tonight I am feeling English," the *Duc* said, "and I am trying to express myself sincerely rather than eloquently."

"I am glad you think the English are sincere."

"I would like to believe they are both sincere and truthful," the *Duc* replied.

He looked deeply into her eyes as he spoke, but she looked away from him.

She had the feeling he was probing; looking down into her very soul; trying to penetrate her facade to find out what she was keeping secret from him.

"It is easy for me to give you a toast," she said to distract his attention.

She raised her glass.

95

"To the Man in the Moon, and may he never cease to shine his light on those who need it!"

"Is that what you think I am doing," the *Duc* asked cynically.

"If you are not, then perhaps it will alert you to your duty," Canéda replied.

She sipped a little of the champagne, then set it down on a small table.

"Do you think Ariel has been stabled all right?" she asked conversationally.

"Are you doubting the hospitality of my stables?" the *Duc* enquired.

"From the outside when I passed them they looked superb," Canéda replied.

"Tomorrow I will show you the inside," the *Duc* said. "I have lately added many modern improvements which I hope will impress you."

"I cannot think they will be better than the stabling we have in England."

"Is your Circus wealthy enough to own stables?"

Canéda realised she had forgotten she was supposed to be permanently with a Circus and had in fact been thinking of the stables at Langstone Park.

"I have seen quite a number of stables that have nothing to do with the Circus," she replied.

"Their owners perhaps had something to do with you?" the *Duc* remarked.

He was speaking in French and it sounded less direct that it would have been in English.

Nevertheless Canéda was annoyed.

"If you mean to be unpleasant, *Monsieur*," she said, "then let me inform you, you have succeeded!"

The *Duc* took her hand in his.

"Forgive me," he said. "It was just that I find you extremely tantalising! Who are you? Why are you here? These are the questions I am going to ask you until I get the right answers."

96

"And when you get the answers what difference will it make?" Canéda enquired.

"That is what is intriguing me."

"I very much doubt it, but at least it will give you something to think about."

"You have given me that already," he said, "and shall I add to what I have already said, that although you bewilder me, I find you entrancing!"

He raised her hand to his lips as he spoke, and once again as he kissed it she felt a strange sensation within her.

It was almost a relief when dinner was announced and they moved once again to the Dining-Room in which they had had luncheon.

Now the curtains were drawn and the big gold candelabra on the table furnished the only light in the room.

It seemed to Canéda as she sat beside the *Duc* that the whole setting accentuated the impression that she was living in a fairy-story.

He certainly did not seem real as he sat back in the huge carved armchair with his coat-of-arms embroidered on the red velvet.

Servants in elaborate livery brought on gold dishes food which was more delicious than anything Canéda had ever eaten in her life before.

The wine and the conversation as dinner progressed made her feel that she was acting on a stage in a play that was so skilfully written that it was difficult to know what would be the end of the Act.

Once again she and the *Duc* were duelling in words and everything they said seemed to have a *double entendre* which made it impossible for them to speak in anything but French.

Only when dinner was finished and the servants left the room did Canéda exclaim:

"That was the most delicious meal I have ever had!"

"I hoped you would say it was one of the most interesting."

"That goes without saying! I enjoyed our conversation more than I can possibly tell you."

"And so have I," the *Duc* said. "How can you be so intelligent?"

"I suppose it is because I have been well educated."

"I do not think that is the real reason."

"Then what is?"

"Because you think. Very few women think except about themselves."

"Is that your experience?"

"It is most men's, and what I am saying, Canéda, is that you are unique."

He had called her by her Christian name ever since they had started dinner, and Canéda thought it would seem rather foolish and pretentious to insist that he addressed her as *'Mademoiselle'*.

She gave him a slightly mocking smile as she answered:

"I am gratified you should think so. I enjoy being different."

"That I can well believe because you *are* different, very different in a way that it is difficult to describe."

"You might say the same about yourself. Of course you are different from other men, and you know it! I think, if you are honest, it is a contrived difference as well as one you were born with."

"Are you accusing me of play-acting?"

Canéda shrugged her shoulders.

"If you like the expression. I think we all act in one way or another."

"Some more than others, as you are acting now," the *Duc* insisted.

"I do not understand why you keep saying that."

"Because it is obvious. You are playing your part very skilfully, but you do not deceive me!"

"Why should I wish to do so?"

"That is for you to say," he said, "and it is what I want to know."

He was again being perceptive, Canéda thought, and that was dangerous.

"Let us go back to the Sitting-Room" she suggested, "and I would like to see what you have written so far about schooling horses. I know it is something that will interest me."

The *Duc* did not reply, he rose as she did and they walked slowly back to the Sitting-Room.

Now the curtains had been closed, the flames from the fire leapt high over the logs, and it looked cosy and romantic.

A servant shut the door behind them and Canéda walked towards the fire and held out her hands in front of it.

"It still gets a little cold at night," she remarked, "I like your big log fires. I was always certain it would be cold on the moon."

She turned her head to smile at him and found that he was standing closer to her than she had anticipated, and there was an expression on his face that made her heart leap.

She straightened herself and he said in a low voice that she could hardly hear:

"You are very lovely – unbelievable so!"

"I am glad you...think...so," she tried to say lightly, but somehow the words seemed almost to stick in her throat.

"I have always believed there was someone like you somewhere in the world," the *Duc* said, "and I must have dreamt of you because I knew today that I had seen you somewhere before."

Canéda felt herself give a little quiver of fear.

She had often wondered if the old *Duc* had a portrait of her mother, for if he had, that was where the present *Duc* would have seen her face.

She did not reply and he went on:

"What am I to do about you? How long can you stay with me, and when you leave me, what will I feel?"

Because he spoke with a seriousness she had not expected and what he said was somehow out of character, Canéda moved a few steps away from him saying:

"I told you I was a shooting-star who had just called in while I was passing. Why should we worry about tomorrow?"

"Why indeed, when we have *tonight*?" the *Duc* replied.

He accentuated the last word, and suddenly Canéda was frightened.

He had not moved, but she put up her hands as if he encroached upon her.

"Please," she said, "let us...talk about our...horses."

"I want to talk about you."

"No...please...no!"

"Why not?"

He moved a little closer to her and now when she would have retreated there was a chair behind her and she could not get away.

"If you are going to be tiresome," she said before he could speak, "I shall be sorry I stayed."

"I do not think that is true," the *Duc* said. "When you were talking at dinner I knew you were enjoying yourself, as I was. And now we are alone, and no-one shall interrupt us."

"You...frighten me," Canéda said in a small voice.

"Why should I do that?"

"I...I do not know...but you...do. Please...please..."

There was silence for a moment. Then the *Duc* said:

"Look at me! Look at me, Canéda! I want to see your eyes."

For some reason she could not explain to herself Canéda knew she should not look at him.

Again she made a little gesture with her hands. Then he said softly, but insistently:

"Look at me!"

It was a command, and like Ariel she could not refuse it.

Because he compelled her to do so, she raised her eyes and looked into his.

For a moment they were both very still. Then it seemed to Canéda as if everything vanished, the room, the candles, the Château, the view outside.

There were only two grey eyes and they filled the whole Universe.

Canéda moved, or the *Duc* did, she only knew that with his eyes holding her, his arms went round her, then his lips held her captive.

Even as he did so, she knew at the back of her mind that this was what she had been wanting and it was at the same time what she had been afraid of – yet it made every moment while she had been with him exciting and thrilling.

She had never been kissed before, but it was exactly as she had thought it would be, and she felt as he drew her closer and still closer to him that they became one and indivisible.

When she became part of the moon itself and there were stars all around them, and there was no world, no problems, no people, only the sky and an ecstasy that enveloped them like a light which came from within themselves, and yet was part of the Divine.

It flashed through Canéda's mind that this was love – love as she had always thought it would be when she found it, but it had always eluded her until now.

It was the love that was so demanding, and yet so utterly and completely perfect that she could not fight it, and there was no escape.

The *Duc* kissed her until she could no longer think, but only feel the wonder of it.

Then as he raised his head Canéda gave a little murmur and hid her face against his neck.

"Now do you understand what I have been trying to say?" he asked very softly.

He was speaking in French, and she thought there was a

tremor in his voice, but she could not be certain.

It was impossible to answer him, she only knew that she felt an incredible rapture pulsating through her body which seemed to end in her throat.

It was in the beat of her heart, and in every breath she drew.

The *Duc* put his hand under her chin and lifted her face up to his.

"There is no need for any questions between us," he said, "you are mine as I knew you were from the very first moment I saw you and thought you had stepped out of my dreams."

His lips were very near to hers as he said again:

"You are mine, Canéda, and I want you! I want you now!"

As he finished speaking his lips were on hers and he was kissing her.

Now there was a fire on his lips that was like nothing Canéda had ever imagined, and yet although it was so fierce and so demanding, she felt herself unaccountably responding to it.

He kissed her until she was breathless, until she felt as if the room spun dizzily around her, and it would be impossible for her to stand unsupported on her feet.

Then he was kissing her neck giving her sensations which she had no idea existed until as her lips parted and her breath came in little gasps, he found her mouth again.

The fire was more intense and she could feel his heart beating against hers.

Then he said, and his voice was hoarse and passionate:

"I want you! God, how I want you! Go and get into bed, my darling. There is no reason for us to wait any longer."

He put his arms around her and drew her across the room.

He opened the door, then because there was a servant in the passage extinguishing the lights in the sconces he took his arm from her.

"I shall not be long," he said very softly, so she could hardly hear the words.

Then he went back to the Sitting-Room shutting the door behind him.

Canéda walked almost as if she was hypnotised down the passage towards her bedroom.

Only as she reached it, did she come back to reality and realise what was happening to her.

It was what vaguely she had sensed might happen, but it had in fact been very different from what she had expected.

And yet, because she had told herself she must be sensible and must on no account take risks with a man she did not know, she had been prepared.

For a moment, as she stood inside the bedroom she thought she could not leave but must stay because she wanted to be with the *Duc*.

Yet what he intended by saying that he wanted her was written in front of her eyes in letters of fire.

Because men had always treated her like a piece of Dresden china, no-one had made such demands before or expressed themselves in such a manner.

She thought the *Duc* would be the same and she would handle him as she had handled the others who had laid their hearts at her feet and pleaded with her to pick them up.

But the *Duc* had just taken possession of her and she knew there was only one answer and that was to go, and go quickly, because she was frightened not only of him, but of herself.

She went to the wardrobe and pulled out a thick cloak in which the maid had wrapped the things she had asked for, so that Ben could carry them on his horse without getting them dirty.

Canéda had, in fact, been surprised to see it, expecting instead a shawl or a linen cover.

The evening cloak was however just what she wanted,

103

and there was no time to change into her riding-habit.

She threw it over her shoulders and opened the bedroom door again very, very cautiously.

There was no sign of the servant who had been extinguishing the lights, and although she was half-afraid to see the *Duc* come from the Sitting-Room she guessed by this time he would have gone to his own bedroom.

Swiftly she sped down the stairs in her soft satin slippers, making hardly a sound until she reached the Hall. A nightwatchman was nodding in a chair by the big door.

"Open the door, please," Canéda said in a voice a little above a whisper in case it should carry.

He looked surprised, but he obeyed her, and as the door began to open she slipped through it and ran across the court-yard and out through the outer door which she had guessed always remained open and which led to the bridge that spanned the moat.

It took her only a few seconds to reach the other side.

Then she saw, as she had expected, that in the shadow of a tree Ben was waiting with two horses.

He was sitting comfortably on the ground and she knew he did not expect her so soon and was prepared to wait, as she had told him to do all night.

Then as she reached him he sprang to his feet.

"Ye be riding as ye are, M'Lady?" he asked.

Canéda did not reply, she merely put her hands on Ariel's saddle and Ben helped her up.

She rode Ariel down the steep incline towards the town.

It was dark, but there were lights in the windows of some of the houses to guide them, and it took only a short while to reach the bridge.

They rode across it, Canéda pressing Ariel on as if the Devil himself was at her heels.

She knew she was running away, not from the *Duc* but from her own heart which inexplicably she had left behind on the moon.

CHAPTER FIVE

Canéda came up on deck to sit in a sheltered spot out of the wind.

The sea was not rough, but there was a heavy swell and *Madame* de Goucourt had retired to her cabin saying she had no intention of breaking her leg.

Canéda was relieved because it meant that she could be alone, and not have to evade the questions which she knew *Madame*, bursting with curiosity, was longing to ask her.

When she had reached the Inn after riding away from the Château, she had gone to her bedroom after giving instructions to Ben.

It was impossible for her to sleep, and when she dressed before her maid came to call her, she knew that *Madame* de Goucourt would have been informed that they were leaving and that by the time they had breakfasted the carriage and the out-riders would be waiting to take them to Bordeaux.

Madame de Goucourt had been astonished at the speed.

"What has happened, Canéda?" she asked when she came to the private room. "Why are we in such a hurry to leave for St. Nazaire?"

"I never intended to stay here for long," Canéda replied evasively.

Madame de Goucourt was an intelligent woman.

She knew by the expression on Canéda's face that something had happened, but as it was obvious she did not wish to speak about it *Madame* forced herself to keep silent, even though it was difficult.

Only when they were driving in the spring sunshine back to Angers did she ask:

"When I received your note yesterday afternoon I thought you were staying the night with friends, but I learned this morning that you returned very late to the Inn."

"It was more convenient for me to do so," Canéda replied.

Even as she spoke she could feel again that moment when she had come down to earth from the heights of ecstasy and realised what the *Duc* intended.

When she had finally got to bed she had lain awake throbbing with the rapture he had evoked in her, even though she tried to deny it.

She had never believed that being kissed could be so ecstatic, so wonderful that she could cease to be herself and become a part of him.

How, she asked, could she have surrendered to him so ignominiously quickly without attempting to struggle?

From the very first moment she had set eyes on him she had known he was different from other men, not only different in his appearance and behaviour, but different in the way he affected her.

None of the men she had met in London who had pursued her, courted her, wooed her and proposed to her had aroused her in any way, except that she found their persistence rather boring when the first interest in having a new admirer had passed.

With the *Duc* she had been tinglingly aware of him from the moment she rode towards him in the Riding-School.

She told herself it was part of her goal and her objective in seeking revenge because of the way his father had treated hers.

But if she was honest she knew that she had forgotten the feud, or even the reason she had come to Saumac, and been concerned only with the relationship between them

106

which had been dangerously attractive from the first few words they had said to each other.

Twisting and turning on the comfortable feather bed, Canéda could see in the darkness only the *Duc's* grey eyes looking into hers, and feel that surging rapture writhing in her breast at the touch of his lips.

"How can I ever forget him?" she asked herself now as she looked out over the green sea.

She wondered what he was feeling and what indeed he had felt when he had gone to her bedroom last night to find it empty.

"He had no right to try to seduce me," she tried to say angrily.

But she knew it had not been a question of seduction but of two people needing and wanting each other, and finding that they belonged in a strange, unearthly manner that it would have been unthinkable to refute.

It was impossible for Canéda not to know that she still wanted him, and that her whole body ached for the feeling of his arms around her and his lips on hers.

"It is just my imagination," she tried to say to herself. "I was amused and enchanted by the Château by the fantasy that I was not on the earth but on the moon, and carried away by the romance of it."

Then she knew that was not true. It was something much deeper and much more fundamental than that.

They were a man and a woman, Adam and Eve, finding each other across eternity and knowing they were no longer two people, but one.

As the yacht sailed on down the coast, Canéda asked herself how she could sink so low as to feel this way for a man who, before she left England, she had hated for what his father had done to her father, just as she hated her grandparents for their treatment of her mother.

"I came to France for revenge," she chided herself, "and I wanted to make him suffer!"

But instead, she knew that she was suffering in a

manner she had never envisaged was possible.

How could anyone make her feel as she did now? Because she loved the *Duc* it seemed as if she had lost something so precious, so wonderful that the world would never be the same again.

It took them two days to reach Bordeaux and to Canéda they were two days of introspection and misery.

She gave up pretending that the *Duc* meant nothing to her, and that in hurting him she had achieved what she had set out to do.

There was no way of ascertaining that he missed her as much as she missed him, and she would lie awake in her cabin thinking that by now he had doubtless consoled himself very adequately with his horses and his – mistress.

The last thought was like the stab of a dagger in her heart and she almost cried out at the pain of it.

Canéda told herself that he had insulted her by suggesting that she should hold the same position in his life.

Yet she had to admit that she had invited such a suggestion by her behaviour, not only in pretending that she was a Circus performer but also in allowing him to kiss her.

What else was he likely to think except that she was a woman with easy morals, especially as she had been prepared to stay alone at the Château?

"I must have been crazy to agree to that!" Canéda whispered, and prayed that Harry would never find out what had happened.

She knew that she had been absurdly naïve in thinking that she could handle any situation that arose, and it was both her innocence and the fact that the *Duc* did not think of her as a Lady that had resulted in a situation of which now she was ashamed.

At the same time, to be in the *Duc's* arms had been the most marvellous and perfect thing that had ever happened to her in her whole life, and she felt with a kind of despair that never again would she be able to feel the same for any other man.

When they sailed into the harbour of Bordeaux it was so interesting and so different from anywhere else she had been in the world that Canéda for a little while forgot her secret unhappiness.

They stayed the night in a comfortable Hotel, giving the horses a chance to recover from the sea passage, before Canéda put her second plan into operation.

First she sent one of the out-riders, resplendently dressed in his best livery ahead to the Château de Bantôme to tell her grandparents she had arrived in her brother's yacht at Bordeaux and was on her way to visit them.

She thought it would be a surprise that their invitation had been answered so quickly, and she instructed the out-rider to inform the *Comte* and *Comtesse* of how many her entourage consisted and what accommodation would be needed for the horses and attendants, besides herself.

It would have been impossible to get all her luggage into the smart travelling-chariot that she had brought with her in the yacht.

She therefore hired the most impressive and expensive carriage available in Bordeaux drawn by four horses to go ahead.

It carried her, her luggage, her lady's-maid, a French-woman whom they had engaged with the help of the Proprietor of the Hotel to wait on *Madame* de Goucourt.

By this time *Madame* was well aware that Canéda intended to impress her relatives and she said with a twinkle in her eye:

"The Château de Bantôme is fortunately large enough to accommodate such an influx of visitors. I am still waiting, *Ma Chérie*, for you to tell me what happened when you met the *Duc* de Saumac."

Canéda started.

"How do you know I met the *Duc*?" she asked defensively.

"I am not stupid," *Madame* de Goucourt replied. "I realised that was why we stayed near Angers which is not far from the Château de Saumac. I also guessed the reason for your disappearance."

"I do not wish to talk about it."

Madame de Goucourt shook her head.

"I am afraid the *Duc* has upset you. You have not seemed yourself since we left Angers. I warned you that he is a very strange man. I think he must loathe all women since his wife went mad."

Canéda wanted to tell her this was not true, but she could not bear to speak of him and after a little silence *Madame* said:

"I will not plague you with questions, *Ma Petite*, but you were so happy when we left England, and now you are suffering."

There was no response and after giving a little sigh she talked of other things.

There was certainly a lot to see that was different from the France Canéda had admired inthe Loire Valley.

When they riched the Dordogne river there had obviously been quite a lot of rain, for it was swollen to what Canéda was sure was almost twice its normal size, as well as there being floods in the fields on either side of it.

The profusion of water made the high cliffs through which the Dordogne passed, even more impressive and there were the Châteaux and the Castles on the summit of them that resembled Saumac.

There also were forests, and dark trees covered hill-tops which were a background to the green valleys.

The trees were all in bloom and with the white black-thorn, golden gorse and beside the roads a profusion of cow-slips, the countryside had a beauty to which Canéda could not help responding.

But all the time she was trying to remember that this was her mother's birthplace, she was conscious of a lump like a heavy stone within her breast which would not go away.

From what she had heard and from what she had read on the map, Canéda knew that the Château de Bantôme was not very far from Bordeaux.

They stayed one night on the way, then they were in Périgord, and *Madame* de Goucourt was full of stories of the old Abbeys – the Cathedrals and the Châteaux they passed.

They drove into wine-growing country, and it seemed to Canéda that those vineyards they passed seemed in good heart, and there appeared to be nothing very wrong with them.

In the afternoon of the second day when they had been travelling for some hours *Madame* de Goucourt pointed ahead and said:

"There is the Château belonging to your grandparents!"

It was about a mile off the road, standing on a steep incline with trees behind it. Built of white stone it was very impressive, and Canéda stared at it with a strange feeling that she had seen it before.

She knew it was because her mother had described it to her so often, and even attempted to draw sketches, to explain to her children what her home looked like.

Canéda knew that the building had been started in the middle of the 16th century and added to and altered by various *Comtes* de Bantôme.

Each owner had embellished and enriched the Château until it looked more like a Palace than a mere nobleman's residence, and its beauty was enhanced by its gardens as well as the dark woods which framed it as if it was a precious jewel.

As they drew nearer they saw there was a fountain playing in front of the house and in the sunshine the water, thrown high in the air, glittered with the colours of the rainbow.

'I can understand why Mama loved it so much,' Canéda thought.

Then she steeled herself to remember that her mother had been exiled from her home and that she hated its occupants, everyone of them!

She hoped her grandparents would be impressed by the magnificent horses drawing her chariot, by the out-riders in their powdered wigs, and by Ben, who had taken the place of the one who had gone ahead, in a smart livery and cockaded top-hat, riding Ariel.

The coachman drew the carriage up with a flourish outside the front door, and servants appeared as if they had been waiting their arrival.

The carriage-door was opened and Canéda stepped out followed by *Madame* de Goucourt.

"You go first," Canéda had said, but *Madame* had shaken her head.

"This is your family you are meeting."

"Do not forget I hate them!" Canéda replied.

"You cannot say that," *Madame* persisted, "until you have met them, and I think, *Ma Chérie*, you are in for a surprise!"

Canéda raised her eye-brows, but there had been no chance to answer for as she walked up the steps of the Château a young man appeared and hurried towards them.

"May I welcome you, Cousin Canéda, on behalf of my grandparents," he asked. "I am Armand!"

He was dark-haired, and attractive, and because he was smiling at her with a very obvious look of admiration in his eyes, Canéda found it difficult not to smile back instead of being cold and imperious as she had intended to be during the whole visit.

She however shook hands with him and presented him to *Madame* de Goucourt who, as he kissed her hand, said:

"I have not seen you since you were six years old, so it is quite unnecessary for me to add that you have grown!"

"I have heard my family speak of you so often, *Madame*," Armand replied, "and everything they have said was of course, complimentary."

He certainly had the right sort of attitude for a French-man, Canéda thought scornfully. Then turning to her he said:

"My grandparents are waiting for you in the Salon. You must forgive their not coming to the door to meet you, but *Grand-père* has difficulty in walking."

Canéda inclined her head and they walked into a very impressive Hall and down a passage that was decorated with very fine antique furniture and pictures that were, she supposed, of the de Bantôme ancestors.

There seemed to be few servants about and it struck her that the place looked a little dull and dusty, as if it was in need not only of cleaning but of painting and decorating.

She tried not to notice that the carpets were threadbare and the curtains at the windows faded and in need of relining.

Armand opened a door and she found herself in a large Salon which overlooked an ornamental garden at the back of the Château.

Seated in the window was an elderly woman with white hair and after one glance at her Canéda felt a sudden constriction in her heart, for the face turned towards her was that of her mother, although older and lined with age.

"Here is Cousin Canéda, *Grand-mère*," Armand announced.

The *Comtesse* held out her hands.

"My dear child!" she exlcaimed. "I cannot tell you how happy I am to see you or what it meant to learn that you had answered my letter so quickly!"

Canéda curtsied, then as she put out her hand the *Comtesse* took it between both hers and pulled her forward.

Canéda had told herself before she left England that nothing would make her show any gesture of affection towards her hated relatives, and yet now it was impossible to avoid the kiss her grandmother gave her on her cheek.

"Sit down, my dear," the *Comtesse* said, indicating a chair beside her.

Then with an undoubted tremor in her voice, she added:

"You are so like your mother, so very, very like her, and I have missed her so much all these years!"

Canéda wanted to reply that the de Bantômes had shown no sign of it, but Armand was presenting *Madame* de Goucourt to his grandmother, before he said:

"I must go and fetch Hélène. She did not expect them to be here so soon."

"Yes, do that, dear boy," the *Comtesse* replied, "and ask the servants to bring refreshments. I am sure they have forgotten."

"I will do that, *Grand-mère*."

He smiled at Canéda before he left and again she had difficulty in not responding.

She sat very stiffly and straight-backed in the chair beside the *Comtesse* and as if she felt her antagonism her grandmother talked to *Madame* de Goucourt, whom she had known for many years.

"I could not believe it was true when the groom came with the message that you had arrived in Bordeaux on your yacht!" she exclaimed.

She hesitated a moment, then she asked Canéda:

"It is your yacht?"

"It belongs to my brother Harry."

"Is that what you call him? I wondered when I saw in the newspapers that he had inherited your uncle's title if you called him Edward. It always seems a rather dull name."

Again Canéda felt antagonistically that if Harry had not come into the title her grandmother would certainly not have written to him and she would not be here at this moment.

The door of the Salon opened, and Armand returned with a very pretty girl.

Canéda could see some resemblance to herself, although of course both Hélène and Armand had dark eyes instead of her sensational blue ones.

She also accepted without conceit that Hélène was not as pretty as she was, because she resembled her mother.

"It is exciting to meet you, Cousin Canéda," Hélène cried, "and I have longed to do so because I have always thought that the way your mother ran away to be married was the most thrilling and romantic story I have ever heard!"

Canéda was astonished that her cousin should speak of it so openly, and in front of the *Comtesse* but she did not miss the opportunity of saying:

"My mother was very, very happy. At the same time she missed her family, and it made her very sad that you all ostracised her for so many years."

Even to think of her mother's suffering made her angry and her voice seemed to ring out in the Salon, and for a moment there was silence.

Then her two cousins looked first at each other, then at the *Comtesse*.

"I can understand, my dear," the old lady said, "that you must feel very bitter that your mother was cut off from those she loved and it hurt me, because she was my daughter, more than I can ever express in words."

"Then why were you so cruel?" Canéda asked bluntly.

The *Comtesse* made a nervous gesture with her blue-veined hands that was very eloquent, but at that moment the door opened and an old man came in supported on either side by servants.

They almost carried him across the room to sit him down in a chair next to the *Comtesse,* putting a fur-lined rug over his knees.

He did not speak, and the *Comtesse* said:

"Françoise, dear, Canéda has arrived. I told you she was coming today."

"Who? Who?" the old man asked.

He had a fine head and must, Canéda thought, have been exceedingly handsome when he was young.

Now his hair was white and his face deeply lined, and yet she had the feeling that the *Comtesse* and his grandchildren were in awe of him.

"Canéda," the *Comtesse* answered. "She is here to visit us from England.

As she spoke she looked at Canéda who realised that her grandmother wanted her to rise and go nearer to the *Comte*.

She did so, pleased that she was wearing an exceedingly expensive and very elegant silk gown with a taffeta pelisse over it and a bonnet trimmed with small ostrich feathers that had been astronomically expensive.

Now she was to meet her grandfather, the relative who she was certain had been more instrumental than anyone else in treating her mother as if she was a leper because she had married the man she loved.

With her chin held high and her back very straight Canéda moved in front of him, and as he stared at her, dropped him a small curtsey.

For a moment there was silence. Then in a voice that sounded strangled, the *Comte* said:

"Clémentine! You are Clémentine!"

"No, dear," the *Comtesse* said quickly, "this is Canéda, Clémentine's daughter."

The old man did not seem to hear her.

"You have come back, Clémentine!" he cried. "That is good! I knew you would see sense. Saumac was distraught because you disappeared. He loves you. I have never known a man so much in love. I had to tell him we could not find you, but now everything will be all right! Everything!"

He smiled and said to his wife:

"Send for Saumac. Tell him Clémentine is here. It will make him happy. Poor man, I was sorry for him. He has been so unhappy!"

Because for the moment it seemed as if the *Comtesse* had no words with which to correct her husband Canéda took the initiative.

She went a little nearer and said:

"Look at me, *Grand-père*. I am not Clémentine but your granddaughter Canéda."

"You are not Clémentine?"

He spoke the words very slowly as if with an effort.

"No, *Grand-père*...my mother...Clémentine is...dead."

It was difficult to say the words, and yet her voice sounded quite clear.

For a moment her meaning did not percolate through to the old man's mind. Then suddenly, in such a loud voice it made her jump, he said:

"What are you saying? Clémentine cannot be dead! She is to marry Saumac. It is all arranged. Where is she? Where has she gone to? What are you keeping from me?"

His voice grew louder and more agitated, and Armand ran to the door.

The two servants who had escorted the *Comte* into the Salon and who were obviously waiting outside came quickly across the room towards him.

"Clémentine! Where is Clémentine?" the old man was shouting as they lifted him from his chair.

"Come along, *Monsieur le Comte*," one of the servants said. "There is a glass of wine waiting for you in your own room."

"I do not want any wine," the old man replied angrily. "I want Clémentine! Where is she? The wedding is tomorrow. The *Duc* will be here tonight and how can we tell him that we cannot find her? Find her, you fools! Find her! She cannot have gone far!"

They were moving him towards the door, and as they went through it he was shouting:

"Clémentine! Clémentine! Where are you, Clémentine?"

Canéda could hear his voice echoing back as they

moved him down the passage.

She stood feeling curiously shaken by what had occurred.

Then as she looked at her grandmother she realised she was holding a handkerchief to her eyes.

"I think you should pour some wine for your grandmother," *Madame* de Goucourt said to Armand in a low voice.

As if glad he could do something Armand went towards the door as two servants came in carrying a silver tray on which there were glasses and small patisseries.

Armand took a glass from the tray and carried it to his grandmother's side.

"Drink this, *Grand-mère*," he said, "and do not be upset."

"He has been better for the last two days," the *Comtesse* said in a low voice, "and I did not want Canéda to know what he was like."

"She would have learned sooner or later," Armand said soothingly, "and I feel she will understand."

He looked at Canéda as he spoke as if he wished she would support him and she said quickly:

"Of course. I am sorry that Mama running away upset him so much."

"He has never been the same since," the *Comtesse* said in a low voice, "sometimes he is his usual self, but with our worries lately he has grown much worse."

"Do not talk about it, *Grand-mère*," Hélène said. "You know it always upsets you, and as this is Cousin Canéda's first visit here we have so much to show her."

"Yes, of course," the *Comtesse* agreed, "and it is stupid of me to be upset."

As she wiped her eyes *Madame* de Goucourt moved closer to her while Canéda rose to walk to the window and look at the formal gardens.

They were laid out in the way that had been made fashionable by the gardens at Versailles.

But even at a quick glance Canéda could see they were not well tended and needed attention.

Hélène and Armand joined her at the window.

Armand offered her a glass of wine. Then he said in a low voice so that his grandmother could not hear:

"I am so sorry you have been involved in a scene so soon after your arrival, but we never thought that *Grand-père* would take you for your mother."

"Is it true," Canéda asked, "that he has been like this since Mama ran away?"

"I have always heard," Armand replied, "that at first he was furiously angry, then very bitter."

"And now?"

"Now with all the other troubles his mind has gone back to the past" Armand said. "He often talks as if he was living twenty years ago, and that is why, if we had had any sense, we would have realised he would think you were your mother."

There was silence, then Canéda had to ask the questions which trembled on her lips.

"Did the *Duc* de Saumac really love Mama?"

"So my mother has always told me," Armand replied.

"Papa said he adored her!" Hélène interposed. "He was much older than she was, but Papa said he was like a young man who falls in love for the first time."

"I expect that was true," Armand said. "After all Cousin Canéda knows that marriages are arranged in France, and it is only the second time round that we have the chance of choosing our wives rather than the family doing it for us."

"Mama thought the *Duc* only wanted to marry her in order to have more children," Canéda said.

"I am sure that was not true," Hélène answered, "it was really all very romantic."

"Tell me what you know," Canéda said.

"The *Duc* saw your mother at a party and fell in love with her, and of course in those days, as now, it was

119

Grand-père who accepted his proposal and I expect your mother was just told she was to be a *Duchesse*."

"Yes, that is true," Canéda agreed.

"We have always heard from our parents that the *Duc* was so deeply in love with her that when she disappeared he nearly went mad and raged at *Grand-père*, then scoured the countryside, and when finally it was known that your father and mother had married, he talked of taking his own life."

"I cannot believe it!" Canéda exclaimed.

"It is true," Armand said. "I have been told the same story, not only by my father and mother, but by dozens of other de Bantômes who were there at the time."

"*Grand-père* had a terrible time with the *Duc* and he too was very unhappy," Hélène said. "He loved your mother, perhaps more than his other children, and I think that was why he could not bear to talk about her or accept that she even existed because she had married an Englishman."

Canéda gave a sigh.

It was all so very different from what she had anticipated, and she knew that the sight of her grandfather, a little mad, calling for her mother, had upset her more than she liked to admit.

When she was taken to her bedroom she noticed again as she walked through the house escorted by Hélène that much of it was shabby and in need of repair.

In her bedroom which was very impressive and was, as Hélène told her, one of the State Rooms, the silk brocade was peeling off the walls in places.

The exquisitely painted ceiling was damaged by damp and the chairs needed recovering.

Hélène saw Canéda's eyes glancing around her and said in a slightly embarrassed way:

"I am afraid there is a great deal that needs doing but, as you will understand, there has had to be drastic economies these last years."

"Are you saying that the de Bantômes are hard up?" Canéda enquired.

Hélène looked at her in surprise.

"Of course we are! Did you not know?"

"Why should I, when we have had no communication with you all these years, except for the letter which arrived some weeks ago asking my brother and me to come and stay."

"*Grand-mère* wrote to you!" Hélène exclaimed.

"Yes. Did you not know?"

"We never heard her mention you until your groom arrived saying you were on your way from Bordeaux."

Canéda looked astonished, then Hélène said:

"I quite understand what has happened. She wants your help."

"That is what she asked for," Canéda said coldly.

Hélène made a little gesture with her hand.

"I suppose we are in such a mess that *Grand-mère* is clutching at any straw, although I am sure Papa and Mama will be as surprised as I am, that she actually asked you to come here."

Canéda had already heard that her mother's brother, René, and his wife, the parents of Armand and Hélène, were in Paris.

Now Hélène said:

"Papa is trying to raise a loan somehow from the Banks or from friends, otherwise I do not know what will happen in the future."

Canéda paused before she asked what she knew was a vital question.

"You grow wine. Are the vines in fact infected with phylloxera?"

Hélène nodded.

"It started five years ago in a small way, but now it is getting worse and worse. There seems to be nothing we can do to stop it."

There was a note in her voice that told Canéda how

much it mattered to her personally.

"Surely there must be some cure?" she asked.

"Only to flood the vineyards but naturally the hill-side cannot be flooded."

"Then what will happen?" Canéda asked.

"For a moment Hélène did not answer. Then she said:

"We will not be able to live here and the Château will have to be closed. I do not know where we shall go, or what Papa will do. All our money comes from the wine."

Canéda could understand why her grandmother had been desperate and had written to Harry.

There was no need for it to be put into words for her to know that without a dowry no Frenchman would want to marry Hélène, and Armand, even though one day he would be the *Comte* de Bantôme, would not be acceptable as a suitor in any family who could provide their daughter with an income.

It was as if she was watching something which had always been strong and stable crumbling to the ground, and she knew how distraught her mother would have been.

"It must not depress you," Hélène said quickly. "It is delightful to have you here, and you are so beautiful! We have always been told that your Mama was the beauty of the family, and now I know that is true. Tomorrow I will show you a portrait of her."

"There is one here in the Château?" Canéda asked eagerly.

"There are several," Hélène said. "They are all hidden away because they upset *Grand-père*, but we will bring them out, and I expect if you ask *Grand-mère* she will let you have one to take back to England with you."

"I would like that," Canéda said simply.

"And I want you to tell me about your mother," Hélène said. "To me, as I have already said, it is the most romantic story I have ever heard, to know that she was brave enough to run away when her wedding-gown was

122

waiting for her, her trousseau was packed, and the house filled with guests and presents."

Canéda smiled.

"She was in love."

"I know," Hélène said. "That is what makes it so marvellous, that love made her brave enough to leave everything to which she belonged – and the *Duc*."

Canéda smiled again.

"When one is in love a title is not important."

"That is what Aunt Clémentine made very clear," Hélène said, "but I am sure if I was going to marry a *Duc* I would never be brave enough to run away with a plain *'Monsieur'*."

"You would do so like my mother, if you found a man who you really loved," Canéda said.

Hélène smiled at her, but Canéda knew she was not convinced.

It was the ambition of every French girl to have a great Château of her own and a social position that was unassailable.

That was exactly what her mother had been offered by the *Duc* de Saumac, yet she had run away with a penniless Englishman without a title and without prospects of ever having one.

It suddenly struck her that if she herself had never met the *Duc* then she would not have really understood why her mother had given up so much.

She had known how happy she was with her father. At the same time she had been well aware of how poor they were and how difficult it was to make ends meet; how hard it was for her father never to have suitable horses to ride.

Some critical part of her mind had made her ask as soon as she was old enough:

"Has it really been worth giving up so much, Mama?"

She had thought not only of the *Duc*, but of the powerful, rich de Bantôme family with their acres of land in Périgord and their magnificent Château.

Sometimes, when she had seen her mother looking at a gown that was out of fashion and almost threadbare and wondering how she could make it last a little longer, she had longed to say:

"How could you, Mama, give up so much for Papa, adorable though he is?"

Now she understood and was frightened to know that she understood only because the *Duc* had kissed her with a strange enchantment that made her forget everything except him.

It flashed through her mind that if the *Duc* had been an almost penniless younger son like her father, and he had asked her to marry him, she would have said 'yes'.

That was love and, although her mind tried to repudiate it, she knew hopelessly, irrevocably, that she loved a man whom she could never marry because he already had a wife.

The *Duc* de Saumac!

CHAPTER SIX

The *Comtesse* put out her hand to draw Canéda down beside her.

"I want you to tell me about your mother, my dear," she said.

Canéda paused for a moment.

Before she had arrived at the Château, she had planned so many things that she would say, but now her whole attitude towards her relatives was changing, especially towards the *Comtesse*.

After a moment she said:

"Mama was very, very happy with my father, but at times she felt homesick for her family, especially you, *Grand-mère*."

She saw the tears come into her grandmother's eyes before she replied:

"And I missed her! One day, when you have children of your own, you will know how much they mean and whether one sees them or not, one never ceases to worry over them and – love them."

There was a throb in her voice that told Canéda how sincere the words were and after a moment a little hesitatingly because she did not wish to be unkind she said:

"How could you have ignored Mama all those years and never communicated with her even when she wrote to you?"

She thought what had hurt her mother more than anything else was that, when she had written to her own mother saying she had a son, the letter had been returned unopened.

The *Comtesse* gave a little cry that was one of pain.

"You must believe me, Canéda," she said, "when I tell you that I had no idea until a long time later that your mother had written to me or that the letter had been returned."

"How is that possible?" Canéda asked.

"Your grandfather was dreadfully upset and angry when she ran away, but I think he might have forgiven her if the *Duc* de Saumac had not been with us so much, raging with anger one moment because he had been made to look a fool over the wedding, then at the next in despair and desolate in a way I cannot describe because he had lost your mother whom he loved."

The *Comtesse* drew in her breath as if it was hard for her to remember how upsetting it had all been.

Then she went on:

"I am convinced the *Duc* was largely responsible for the fact that your grandfather became a little unbalanced and it was impossible for any of us to mention your mother's name without there being a scene."

Canéda was silent, thinking that her mother had imagined they had just forgotten her and wiped her out of their lives.

"Your grandfather's secretary, who had been with us for many years and who was devoted to him, was deeply upset at what was happening, and when your mother's letter came he sent it back without telling either me or your grandfather that it had arrived."

"How could he do such a thing?" Canéda asked indignantly.

"He thought he was saving us more pain and misery," the *Comtesse* replied. "I have often thought that good wishers do more harm than good."

"Mama wrote to tell you that she had a son," Canéda said.

"How I wish I had known," the *Comtesse* murmured.

Now the tears welled up in her old eyes and ran down her cheeks.

Impulsively Canéda put out her hand to hold hers.

"I do not want you to be upset," she said, "and I promise you Mama was blissfully happy even though we were very poor. In fact, I often thought my home radiated with sunshine all the year round."

"She never regretted the social position she had thrown away?" the *Comtesse* asked.

Canéda shook her head.

"I do not think Papa or Mama would have changed their lives in any way, even if they had been offered the position of King and Queen!"

As she spoke Canéda thought that was exactly what love meant, and she was understanding for the first time that nothing that the world could offer was more wonderful or more perfect than to be in the arms of the man one loved.

Because her whole being cried out for the *Duc* she said quickly:

"I want to tell you about my home, *Grand-mère,* and what fun Harry and I had as children, and while I am here I want to show you the tricks my horse Ariel can do."

She then told her grandmother how her father and she had brought Ariel from the Circus and all the time she related the story she was thinking of how she had told it to the *Duc*.

She could see his grey eyes looking at her as he listened intently, and she felt again that strange, magnetic vibration between them which had made her so tinglingly conscious of him even before she knew that she loved him.

When Canéda finished there was a smile on her grandmother's lips and she said:

"Thank you, dear child, you have told me so much that I have always longed to know. And now, what about yourself? You are nineteen. It is time your brother arranged your marriage."

"I assure you I would never marry a man I did not love," Canéda replied quickly.

Even as she said the words in the same way as she might have said them to Harry, she knew forlornly that if that was true then she would never marry.

How could she ever feel for another man as she felt for the *Duc?* And yet how could she face a life of being an old maid, an aunt in the future to Harry's children, without any of her own?

The thought made her want to cry out in misery, and because she wished to escape from her thoughts she kissed her grandmother and went in search of Armand with whom she had promised to ride later in the afternoon.

He was waiting for her, and when they set off it was inevitable that as soon as they left the Park they should come to the vineyards.

There was devastation where the vines had been uprooted because they were diseased.

This had obviously happened very recently in one place where the roots were being burnt so that there were dozens of little fires, their smoke rising on the still air.

There was something deeply depressing about it, Canéda thought, and without even looking at Armand and the men who were working on the vines she knew that the future for them held nothing but despair.

As they rode back to the Château she told herself that the sooner she returned to England the better.

She could feel the de Bantômes' worries and troubles encroaching upon her, and as they combined with her own unhappiness about the *Duc,* she had the uneasy feeling that now the sunshine had gone out of her life and it would be hard to recapture it.

"I must tell *Grand-mère* that I have to make plans to leave," she said to Armand, "perhaps the day after tomorrow or the day after that."

"I shall be very sorry to see you go," he replied. "You have made *Grand-mère* very happy, and Hélène and I are so delighted to have met you. Surely you can stay until Papa and Mama return from Paris?"

"I promised my brother I would not be away for long," Canéda answered automatically.

Then because she knew it was something he wanted to hear she said:

"I know *Grand-mère* wants you and Hélène to come to London, and this evening I will talk to her about it."

She saw Armand's face light up. Then he said:

"That is very kind of you, but probably we shall not be able to afford it."

He did not wait for her answer, but spurred his horse ahead as if he was embarrassed, and Canéda had to make Ariel gallop to keep up with him.

When they got back to the Château she changed her gown and after telling the maid that she could begin packing, she went in search of her grandmother.

The *Comtesse* was sitting, as Canéda had expected with *Madame* de Goucourt in the Salon, with the sunshine coming through the window and Canéda guessed by the expressions on their faces as she came into the room, that they had been talking about her.

As they were both French she was quite certain they were telling each other that a marriage should be arranged for her, and it struck her how shocked they would both be if they knew that the only man who mattered to her was already married.

She walked towards them and the *Comtesse* held out her hand.

"You enjoyed your ride, my dear?"

"It was delightful!" Canéda answered.

She did not mention to her grandmother how horrified she had been at the sight of the vineyards, for she had the feeling that the place where the vines were being burnt was a new disaster and the tragedy had not yet been reported at the Château.

She wondered how extensive the de Bantôme estate

was, and although she tried not to seem too curious she was sure that practically none of it would produce drinkable wine this year and perhaps for many years to come.

She sat down beside her grandmother and *Madame* de Goucourt who was just starting an amusing story of what had happened to her husband the first time he was granted an audience with the Queen at Windsor Castle, when the door opened.

One of the old servants, who were all slightly deaf and therefore shouted when they spoke, announced in a loud voice:

"Monsieur le Duc de Saumac, Madame!"

For a moment Canéda thought she could not have heard him correctly.

Then as the *Duc* came into the Salon she froze into immobility.

He seemed even taller and better looking than she remembered, and it was impossible to breathe as he walked across the room towards her grandmother.

"Léon, my dear boy!" the *Comtesse* exclaimed. "This is indeed a delightful surprise! Why did you not let me know you were in this part of the world?"

"I came unexpectedly," the *Duc* replied after he had kissed the *Comtesse's* hand.

"I do not think you know *Madame* de Goucourt?" the *Comtesse* said.

"Enchanté, Madame!" the *Duc* replied, and raised her hand to his lips.

"And my granddaughter," the *Comtesse* went on, indicating Canéda on the other side of her: "Lady Canéda Lang!"

The *Duc* bowed and there was not a flicker of recognition in his eyes.

Canéda could hardly believe it had happened, but it had!

Without even glancing again in her direction, he sat down in a chair opposite the *Comtesse,* and said:

"How are you? And how is the *Comte*?"

The *Comtesse* shook her head.

"Not very well, I am afraid. But he will be glad to see you, as he always is. Will you be staying with us?"

"I am afraid not," the *Duc* replied. "I have come here especially to see the *Comte* de Menjou about his vineyards."

"Vineyards!"

The exclamation seemed to come from the depths of the *Comtesse's* heart and she added:

"You have a solution to our problem?"

"I believe so," the *Duc* replied.

"What is it?"

"It involves first flooding, then injecting carbon bisulphide into the earth around the roots, and grafting onto existing roots."

"This will prevent the disease spreading?"

"I think so," the *Duc* replied, "but the treatment is expensive."

The *Comtesse* gave a deep sigh, and there was no need for her to say if that was so they could not afford to experiment.

"I do not want to worry you about it," the *Duc* said, "but I will discuss it with your Manager. All the vineyard-owners in this area are meeting tomorrow to decide what is the best thing to do."

"That is kind of you, Léon," the *Comtesse* said, "but please do not speak of it to my husband."

"No, of course not," the *Duc* replied. "It would be a great mistake to cause him more worry than he has already."

"I knew you would understand."

The *Duc* rose to his feet.

"I will go and see him now. I know this is a good time of the day."

"But you will dine with us?" the *Comtesse* cried.

"I would like to do that," the *Duc* answered. "I have my

131

clothes and my valet with me, and perhaps you would be kind enough to send a groom to tell the *Comte* that I will not reach him until after dinner."

"Yes, yes, of course," the *Comtesse* said. "You know your way to my husband's room."

The *Duc* bowed to the *Comtesse* and *Madame* de Goucourt, completely ignoring Canéda, and went from the Salon.

She felt as if she had been holding her breath all the time he had been there, and now he had gone she could hardly believe he had actually been sitting where she could see him.

She had heard his voice and felt as she always did the vibrations emanating from him, and yet he had ignored her!

She knew he had done it to punish her because she had deceived him, or perhaps because he was so shocked at the way she had behaved he had no wish even to speak to her again.

Then she was sure that he must have known she was here before he arrived, otherwise it would have been impossible for him to enter the Salon and not show a flicker of surprise.

After thinking of him so much she had now seen him again! Her heart was thumping in her breast and she wanted, as she had never wanted anything in her life before, to run after him and ask him what he had felt when she had left him, and if he had been disappointed.

She had the terrifying feeling that instead of being disappointed he had just been very angry, and now perhaps he hated her.

She had learned from Harry how much a man disliked being made a fool of by a woman, and there was no doubt that was what she had done when she had pretended to be a Circus performer and allowed him most reprehensibly to kiss her.

Then having excited him as she had originally planned

132

to do, she had just disappeared.

"How can he ever forgive me?" Canéda asked herself despairingly.

* * * * * *

The *Duc* had not returned to the Salon before Canéda went upstairs and she wondered what he was talking about for so long to the *Comte*.

Perhaps her grandfather was telling him that Clémentine had returned.

Even if he did not mention it, the *Duc* would be aware by this time who she was, and that it was her mother who had run away on the eve of her marriage to his father.

Because he was extremely intuitive she felt sure he would now understand why she had behaved as she had, and that she had come to Saumac in search of revenge.

At the same time, she could not be certain of anything, except that he was here, and he obviously did not want to speak to her.

"I must talk to him! I must try to make him understand," she told herself.

Then she thought despairingly that she had behaved in an outrageous manner towards a man who was married to somebody else whom she had deliberately provoked into kissing her and enticed him into making a proposition which he would never have made had he known who she really was.

Then she had run away in what seemed an ignominious fashion.

Because she was ashamed, and also afraid, Canéda considered whether she should not go down to dinner, but say she was ill and retire to bed.

Then she told herself she must see the *Duc* again, even if he would not speak to her and ignored her as he had done before.

At least she could look at him and perhaps for the last time, she would be near him.

She felt her love for him well up inside herself uncontrollably, and she had a feeling that by the end of the evening it would be intensified until she would suffer even more than she had suffered already.

'It is my own fault,' she thought wistfully, but that was no consolation.

She took a long time in choosing for herself one of her prettiest gowns, but certainly not the pink one in case he thought she was deliberately trying to remind him of when they had dined togther.

Instead she chose a gown that was white with a sash and little bows of velvet ribbon that echoed the blue of her eyes.

It was a gown that made her look very young, and when she regarded her reflection in the mirror, she thought perhaps it might seem an excuse for her behaviour.

Then she knew she had not talked to him as if she was young, inexperienced and innocent.

She had deliberately tried to appear worldly-wise and experienced in many things including love.

It struck her that perhaps he would suppose she had behaved with him as she had with other men she met, and she longed to tell him that was not true, that he was the only man who had ever kissed her and the only man she had ever wanted to do so.

She was so agitated by the time she was ready to go downstairs that it was hard to keep herself from trembling.

As she slowly descended the staircase holding onto the banisters she saw a carriage outside the door and several people getting out of it.

It was then she remembered that Hélène had told her there was to be a dinner-party tonight for some of the de Bantôme relatives who had come to meet her.

This, Canéda knew, would make it even more difficult to speak to the *Duc* alone, and she wished that she had gone down earlier, and perhaps had a chance of talking to him before anyone else arrived.

When she entered the Salon it was to find quite a number of people there already and, while they were strangers to her, they all appeared to know the *Duc* well.

They sat down eighteen to dinner and it all looked very glamorous because the lighted candelabra on the table obscured the parts of the room that needed redecorating.

The *Duc* was seated on her grandmother's right at the end of the table and she found herself placed betwen two elderly but important cousins who had come specially to meet her.

She could not hear what the *Duc* said, but she watched him talking to her grandmother and to the wife of another de Bantôme cousin. She knew he did not give a single glance in her direction, and as far as he was concerned she did not even exist.

While her cousins paid her compliments she found it hard to respond to them politely, and because her thoughts kept straying to the *Duc* they often had to repeat what they had said before it percolated through to her mind and she was able to answer them.

"I must speak to him...I must!" Canéda told herself frantically, as in French fashion the ladies and gentlemen left the Dining-Room to proceed back to the Salon.

It was now dark and the chandeliers had been lighted.

Her grandmother had resisted putting in new forms of lighting. However the candlelight was very becoming, and seeing how attractive all the other women looked, Canéda was aware that she herself was looking her best.

She tried to edge her way to the side of the *Duc* and just when she had nearly achieved it without appearing obvious, she heard him say to her grandmother:

"I know you will forgive me, *Madame*, if I say good-night and thank you for a most delightful evening. As you are well aware the *Comte* de Menjou is not as young as he was, and I do not like to feel I am keeping him up late."

"No, of course not, Léon," the *Comtesse* replied. "It was delightful to see you. Will you come again tomorrow or another day before you leave?"

"Tomorrow I am going to Paris," the *Duc* said.

"You are lucky!" Armand exclaimed who had been listening to the conversation. "That is where I want to go."

"There will be plenty of time yet for you to enjoy the frivolities of Paris," the *Duc* answered.

The way he spoke made Canéda know only too well what the word 'frivolities' meant to him and to Armand, who looked sulky because he had to stay at home.

The *Duc* kissed the *Comtesse's* hand and turned to say goodbye to *Madame* de Goucourt.

Canéda held her breath.

She was next to *Madame* and she knew it would be impossible for the *Duc* to pretend not to see her.

"*Au revoir, Madame,*" the *Duc* was saying. "It has been delightful to see you again, and I hope our next meeting will not be delayed for so long."

"So do I," *Madame* laughed, "and if it is, then you will not have grown taller, but older."

"Which, of course, is something to be avoided," the *Duc* replied.

'Now,' Canéda thought to herself, 'now he will have to speak to me.'

Her hand was ready. Then to her consternation the *Duc* turned completely round to face in the opposite direction.

He made it appear quite a natural movement, as if he wanted to speak to one of the de Bantôme cousins whom he obviously knew well.

But she knew it was a deliberate action on his part to avoid her.

Then he said goodbye to several other people in the Hall and the door closed behind him.

For a moment Canéda contemplated running after him regardless of what anyone might think.

Then she knew that even so there would be no chance of a private conversation, for not only was Armand with him to see him off, but the servants were waiting in the Hall.

And what could she say – except goodbye?

She was quite certain he would be as formal and indifferent as he had appeared so far.

Because she loved him she could hardly believe that her feelings had not communicated themselves to him. He must have been aware of how she had yearned for the touch of his hand and to see his eyes looking into hers.

Then she knew it was finished, finished and over – the most exciting and the most thrilling and wonderful adventure in her life.

She had met a man who was different from all the other men, and to whom she belonged, whether he wanted her or not.

He had said she was his, but he had not meant it, except as an expression of desire for someone he had found excited him physically.

But for her it was a spiritual union which nothing could break.

His kiss had carried her towards the sky, and it was there in what they had called the moon she had known that she was his and he was hers and spiritually they were indivisible.

"I will never see him again," Canéda said to herself later that night, "but I shall always belong to him with my heart and soul, and that is something I can never give to any other man."

She felt she was running away again, but this time from France because it was associated with the *Duc* and she could only pray that when she was home in a different environment she would not miss him so desperately as she did at this moment.

The stone that seemed to be in her heart was heavier than ever, and she thought she would never be free of it. It would break her and take away the joy of living for ever.

* * * * * *

All the preparations had been made for Canéda to leave, and as they had to start early in the morning to reach the town where they were to stay that night, she went to say goodbye to her grandmother in her Boudoir.

She had said goodbye to her grandfather. He had been quieter when she went to see him in his room, and although he called her 'Clémentine' he had not spoken of the *Duc* or talked of the vineyards and how worried he was that on one or two of them there were signs of phylloxera.

Armand had already told Canéda that they had kept from the old man the extent of the damage, and Canéda had cheered him up.

"There are some new ideas on how the vines can be cured of the disease," she said.

"Who told you this?" her grandfather asked.

Canéda hesitated a moment before she replied:

"The *Duc* de Saumac, *Grand-père*. And if he says there is a cure, you may be certain there will be. He is a very clever man."

"You will be lucky, my dear, to have such a brilliant husband."

He put out his hand to pat Canéda's as he said:

"I know how happy you will both be together."

He paused before he continued:

"I have often been clairvoyant about certain things, especially in regard to my own family, and I can tell you, my dearest daughter, as clearly as if I could see it written down in front of me, that you and the *Duc* will have an ideal marriage."

Canéda drew in her breath.

"I...hope you are...right...*Grand-père*," she said in a low voice.

"I know I am right," the *Comte* insisted. "You will be very happy as few people have the good fortune to be, and do not forget – call your first son after me. That would please me."

"I will do that, *Grand-père*."

Canéda kissed the *Comte* goodbye, and as she reached the door of the room she heard him saying to himself:

"You are a good girl, Clémentine, and you will be happy as we have always wanted you to be."

Outside the door she stood for a moment fighting for composure before she returned to the Salon.

If only what her grandfather had said was true: that she was really going to marry the *Duc* and his vision of the future was not just a part of his poor, troubled brain.

Then she told herself that she had to be brave, that life had to go on, and no amount of wishing could change the fact that she could not marry the *Duc* anyway, for even if he was free, he would not want her.

Now, a she knocked on her grandmother's door, she thought of how different her feelings were from what she had expected them to be when she had originally left England.

She had tried to avenge herself on the *Duc* but the person who had been hurt was not him but herself.

She had come here hating her de Bantôme relatives and wanting to humiliate them, but instead she loved them.

"Come in!" she heard the *Comtesse's* voice saying and found her sitting dressed in a négligée having had her breakfast before she dressed to go downstairs.

The old lady held out her hands to Canéda saying:

"I wish you did not have to leave us, dear child. It has been such joy to have you here. I shall miss you when you have gone."

"I shall miss you too, *Grand-mère*," Canéda said and knew it was the truth.

"There is one thing I forgot to tell you," the *Comtesse* said, "and you must forgive me for not mentioning it until now."

"What is it?" Canéda enquired.

"Your mother had some money left her in her own right, but when she ran away your grandfather quite

139

wrongly I think, prevented it from leaving France."

"I know that," Canéda said.

"Then it makes it easier for me to tell you," the *Comtesse* went on, "that it is now yours, and of course, you will understand that as it has accummulated over the years and your grandfather invested it not in vines, but in Railways and other businesses which have made large profits, it now amounts to a very considerable sum of money!"

The *Comtesse* took an envelope from a table beside her and handed it to Canéda.

"There is a letter from our Solicitors which explains about the investments and what is actually in the Bank. Perhaps you will take it with you to Harry and he will understand what to do about it."

Canéda did not take the envelope. Instead she said:

"Listen, *Grand-mère*, I know that Mama if she was alive, would want more than anything else, to help you during this crisis over the vineyards."

She saw a sudden light in her grandmother's eyes and went on:

"I am speaking for Harry and myself when I say that we have been very lucky and this money is far more important to you than it is to us. Spend it on maintaining the estate and keeping the Château in existence."

"Do you really mean that?" the *Comtesse* asked in a strangled voice.

"I mean it," Canéda said, "and shall I add that it comes to you from Mama with her love, which she never ceased to give you."

Tears ran down the *Comtesse's* lined cheeks, but her eyes were shining as she exclaimed:

"Thank you, my dearest child, thank you, thank you! You cannot know what a weight this will be off my mind. I could not bear to have to close the Château and to dismiss so many old servants who would be unable to get work elsewhere."

Canéda kissed the old lady. Then she said:

"Goodbye, *Grand-mère* and send Héléne and Armand to London. I know that I can persuade Harry to give a Ball for them at Langstone House, and after that they will be asked to innumerable Balls, and Iknow Hélène will be a great success."

"How can you be so kind and so forgiving?" the *Comtesse* asked in a broken voice.

Canéda did not answer, she only kissed her grandmother again, finding it hard to keep her own tears from falling.

Then she went downstairs to tell Hélène about the Ball and to know as they drove away that both she and Armand were tremendously excited at the thought that they would all meet again very shortly.

"I hope Cousin Harry will let me ride his horses!" was the last thing Armand said as the carriage moved away from the front door.

"I am sure he will," Canéda replied, and she was laughing as they set off down the drive and waved until the Château was out of sight.

As she leaned back against the comfortable cushions she asked *Madame* de Goucourt:

"Do men ever think of anything but horses?"

"Sometimes they think of women," *Madame* de Goucourt replied.

"Only if they are Frenchmen!" Canéda replied. "With the English, horses come first and women a very poor second!"

"Now you are being cynical!" *Madame* complained. "Moreover seeing you with Ariel, I have rather suspected that you love him more than you love any man!"

"Canéda knew if she told the truth she would have added: "All men except for one!" but aloud she said:

"Ariel is far more intelligent than most men, and certainly more amenable."

"I see I shall have to find you a Centaur as a husband,"

Madame smiled.

This instantly conjured up a picture of the *Duc* riding the chestnut horse over the jumps with an expertise that made him the best rider Canéda had ever seen.

There were so many things he might be, but to her he was always the Man in the Moon, and just as unattainable.

* * * * * *

The yacht was waiting for them at Bordeaux and as they sailed out into the open sea Canéda said goodbye to France.

The visit to the land to which her mother had belonged had been an experience that was quite different from what she had expected, and which she would never forget.

But while she had gone to inflict wounds on other people, it was she herself who had been stricken, and she thought the scars would remain with her all her life.

It would be hard to forget her grandfather, still worried and distressed over a marriage that had not taken place twenty years ago; her grandmother weeping for a daughter she had lost.

What was more, Canéda thought, she and Harry had lost something very precious by being strangers to the family whose blood flowed through their veins.

Still more bitter, she had lost her battle with the *Duc* and was in fact vanquished and annihilated.

The tables had been turned, she had not wreaked her vengeance on him, but he on her.

She cried despairingly at night as the yacht sailed, slowly because the wind was against them, seemingly reluctantly back towards England, and she became more and more convinced that she had left her happiness behind.

But more than that, Canéda thought, she had lost the enchantment she had found in the Château de Saumac, and which she had called the Corner of the Moon.

It was something which persisted in everybody when they were young, when the world was peopled not only by humans, but with dreams, when there was the anticipation of adventure lurking everywhere and the sun rose every morning on a new day to herald the promise of untold rapture.

That had all gone!

Instead there was of course a comfortable, conformable life waiting for her and money to spend which she had never had before, and doubtless a great many men to admire her.

But something was missing; something so vital, so important that without it she was only half of herself, and the half she had lost would be for ever imprisoned in the moon until stars ceased to shine.

CHAPTER SEVEN

Driving along the dusty country lanes towards Langstone Park Canéda did not see the spring buds in the hedgerows, the primroses and cowslips on the banks or the blossom on the trees in the orchards.

Instead she felt as if she was encompassed by a fog of depression because she was leaving France behind her.

The sea had been rather rough after they left Bordeaux, but she had been so busy helping Ben with the horses that she did not have a great deal of time to think about herself.

When finally she got to bed that night she was so tired that she slept from sheer exhaustion, and the next morning she was up early to let Ben have a few hours rest while she calmed the horses.

Ariel was easy, and so was Black Boy, but the carriage-horses and those that had been ridden by the out-riders were frightened when the yacht pitched and tossed, and whimpered when it rolled

Canéda's voice, like Ben's, kept them from panicking, but still it was a relief that the sea was smoother when they reached the Channel.

Just before they sailed into Folkestone Harbour *Madame* de Goucourt had said to Canéda:

"Are you going to Langstone Park, *Ma Chérie*?"

"I will go there first," Canéda replied, "but if Harry is in London I shall join him there."

Madame de Goucourt hesitated a moment. Then she said:

"Would you think it very remiss of me if I left you at

Folkestone and took a train for London?"

"No, of course not," Canéda replied, "and if you are worried about looking after me, I shall be perfectly safe with Ben and the rest of the servants."

"I was reckoning that if I left Folkestone very early I should be at home early in the afternoon."

"Yes, of course," Canéda replied, "and if you want to go to London, of course you must."

"Actually it is my daughter's birthday tomorrow," *Madame* de Goucourt said, "and before I left I told her that there was no likelihood of my being with her. Now, if I catch the early morning train I can be in London for the family luncheon that is being given by her parents-in-law and she was very anxious for me to dine with her and her husband in the evening."

"Then of course you must go," Canéda said.

She thought as she spoke that *Madame* de Goucourt's daughter was lucky to have a family.

It was what she and Harry had missed ever since her father and mother had died.

Now, having been with the de Bantômes she realised how comforting it was, besides being fun, to be a member of a large family.

Madame de Goucourt had said goodbye affectionately to Canéda early that morning, and looking very elegant had set off for Folkestone Station.

Before she left she said:

"You did not confide in me, *Ma Chérie*, but I have the idea that your heart is aching. I wish I could help you, but remember, time heals everything."

Canéda did not reply, but she knew that where she was concerned, time would not heal the ache in her heart, nor would it alter her conviction that she had found the one man who mattered in her life and lost him.

She remembered her mother saying so often that as soon as she met Gerald Lang she had known that nothing else mattered; her social position had been forgotten, the wealth and power that would be hers on marriage, or even that she must hurt the family to which she belonged.

Love had swept everything away except the knowledge that she belonged to Gerald Lang, and he to her.

"It would not have mattered," she had said to Canéda, "if your father had been a poor beggar, or an insignificant bourgeoise. He was the man that God intended for me since the beginning of time, and it was impossible to deny my heart."

There was a deep note of emotion on her mother's voice that told Canéda that even after all the years that had passed and the difficulties they had encountered through having so little money, she never regretted for one moment the drastic step she had taken in running away on the eve of her marriage.

"I think you were very brave, Mama," Canéda had said, and her mother had smiled.

"Not brave, darling, it was a case of self-preservation. Without your father I knew everything that mattered in life would be lost."

That, Canéda knew, was what she was feeling now, a feeling of loss and emptiness, and the stone in her breast seemed to grow heavier as everything around her was very English while her thoughts were in France.

As she drove down the drive towards Langstone Park, for the first time the impressive beauty of the house ceased to thrill her.

Instead of the exquisite and grandiose design by Vanbrugh of the stone steps leading up to a colonnaded front door, all she could see was the four towers of Saumac, silhouetted against the sky which she and the *Duc* had named 'the moon'.

The carriage drew up at the front door and the footman came running down the steps to open the door.

Canéda stepped out and paused to thank the coachman for bringing her home and to smile at Ben who was still seated on Ariel, waiting to ride him round to the stables.

Then slowly, as if she regretted that the journey was over and she was home again, she walked up the steps.

"Welcome home, M'Lady!" the Butler said respectfully.

"How is everything, Dawson?" Canéda asked. "Is His Lordship here or in London?"

"His Lordship's at the stables, M'Lady. I'll send someone to tell him you've returned."

"Yes, please do that," Canéda replied.

She walked up the stairs as she spoke to her own room.

Ben had sent one of the out-riders ahead of them early in the morning, so that she would be expected, and her lady's-maid was waiting for her in her bedroom.

"It's nice to have you home, M'Lady," she said, "and I'm sure you're glad to be back."

"Yes, of course," Canéda replied.

"I hopes Ellen looked after you properly."

"She did her best," Canéda replied.

She took off her travelling-clothes and put on a gown that she had not taken with her.

It was a very pretty one, but she hardly gave herself a glance in the mirror.

What did it matter what she looked like when the one person she wished to admire her was not only hundreds of miles away, but even if he were here would refuse to look at her?

Then she told herself sharply that this was a ridiculous way to think: she had to take up her life in England where she had left it and enjoy herself as she had before.

There would be dozens of men waiting to admire her when she reached London, and she had not been surprised to notice a large number of letters waiting for her on the desk in her bedroom.

Her lady's-maid saw her glance at them and said:

"I'm sure you've been missed in London, M'Lady. Most of those letters were brought down by His Lordship when he came home two days ago, and he told Mr. Barnett that

147

dozens of bouquets of flowers had been delivered to the house, but as Your Ladyship weren't there, they had just wilted away."

Canéda drew in her breath.

"We will go back to London as soon as His Lordship wishes," she said.

She knew it would be the wise thing to do. Nothing could be more foolish than to sit moping at Langstone Park, and worse than anything else, to be alone with her thoughts.

What was the point of remembering what she had felt when the *Duc* had kissed her? Or of recapturing in her mind the wonder and glory when he swept her up into the sky?

She had thought that she would never come down to earth again.

Then she could see his face, stern and unsmiling when her grandmother had introduced him, and after that he had never seemed to look at her again.

She wanted to cry out at the pain of it. Then she asked herself again — "What is the use?"

When she went downstairs hoping that Harry by now would be in from the stables, she felt the same words repeat and repeat themselves over and over again in her mind.

"What is the use?"

What was the use of anything? What was the use of being unhappy? Of crying for the moon? For that was what she was doing.

She walked into the room where she and Harry sat when they were alone.

It was not as formal as the big Drawing-Room but was a delightful Sitting-Room known as 'The Blue Room' which had long French windows opening into the gaarden.

The pictures were not of the more austere Lang relations, but of their children.

There were children looking rather stiff and wide-eyed,

as they posed for the artist, there were children playing with their dolls, and one child holding two small kittens in her arms who looked, Canéda thought, not unlike herself.

She certainly had blue eyes which were characteristic of the Langs, and Canéda had often thought in the past that she would like to have a large number of children who combined her mother's dark hair and her father's blue eyes, which were so sensational in her own face.

She thought now it would be unlikely that she would ever have any children, and if she did they would not be born of love such as her father and mother had for each other.

"What is the use of thinking such stupid things?" she asked herself angrily.

She walked across the room to look out into the garden and forced herself to think how beautiful it was with the lilacs coming into bloom and syringa scenting the air.

Because it was so beautiful, while at the same time she knew despairingly it did not move her, as it would have done a few weeks ago, she felt the tears prick her eyes and told herself it was because she was tired.

"It was a long journey, the sea was rough, and I have not slept very well," she excused herself.

She heard the door open and forced a smile to her lips.

"I am back, safe and sound, as you see Harry..." she began and turned round to feel the words swept from her lips.

It was not Harry who had come into the Sitting-Room but the *Duc*.

He was looking so familiar in his breeches, boots and grey whip-cord riding-coat just as she had seen him after she had jumped into the Riding-School, that for a moment she thought he must be a ghost and that she was imagining him.

Then as he walked towards her she watched him wide-eyed and said quickly:

"W...why are you...here?"

149

"I came to see your brother."

Canéda felt as if she had stopped breathing. Then because she was frightened she asked frantically:

"Why? What had you to...say to him? You...did not...tell him...?"

Her voice died away because the *Duc* had reached her side, and now she was palpitatingly aware of him, acutely conscious that he was near her.

"I certainly told your brother that we had met," the *Duc* said quietly.

"Why should you...want to do...that?"

"I have my own reasons for doing so."

"Harry will be very...angry with me...if you told him..."

There was no mistaking the agitation in her voice.

It swept through Canéda almost like a streak of lightning how furious Harry would be if the *Duc* told him how she had pretended to belong to a Circus!

Worse still, that she had dined alone with him and promised to stay the night!

As if the *Duc* was following her thoughts he said quietly:

"I have not told your brother any of the things that are making you afraid."

Canéda felt her relief almost make her feel weak. Then she asked:

"Why did you come to...see Harry...and why are you in...England?"

"The answer to both questions is the same."

As if she suddenly remembered how much he had hurt her at the Château de Bantôme she turned her face away from him to look out into the garden.

"I cannot understand why you should come here," she said in a voice she tried to make cold and distant, "when you were so...rude to me when we last...met."

"I was punishing you," the *Duc* said, "as you tried to punish me."

Canéda was surprised, but she did not speak and he

150

went on:

" 'An eye for an eye, and a tooth for a tooth.' Was that not the reason why you came to Saumac?"

"How did you...find out...where I...was?"

She was not looking at him, but she knew he smiled.

"It was not very difficult," he said. "The Inn-Keeper where you stayed was very impressed, not only with the two very elegant ladies who stayed in his Hostelry, but with their magnificent horses."

"He told...you that we had gone...back to Angers?"

"At Angers they told me you had gone to Nantes and from Nantes to St. Nazaire."

"Then you...knew who...I was?"

"Of course!" the *Duc* said. "Very large yachts belonging to English noblemen are not so frequent in St. Nazaire, that the inhabitants are not curious about them. In fact, it was the Harbour Master who informed me you had left for Bordeaux."

"Then you guessed where I was going."

"The way your mother treated my father was, of course, something I have never been able to forget."

"And did you...hate Mama as your...father...did?"

"I never hated her," the *Duc* sharply. "I was merely aware that when he lost her he had lost the one thing that mattered to him in his life."

There was silence, then as Canéda did not speak he said very quietly:

"The same thing happened when you went away, and I found you had gone!"

"Canéda felt a little tremor run through her. Then as he said no more she asked in a very small voice:

"Were you...very...angry?"

"I was not angry, but distraught," the *Duc* replied, "I thought I would never be able to find you again."

"And when you did...you were cruel and unkind."

"I am glad you felt like that."

"Why? Because you were having your...revenge

151

on…me?"

"No," he answered, "because if I could hurt you, it meant that you cared."

Canéda felt it would be humiliating for him to know how much she cared, and how unhappy she had been.

With an effort she managed to say:

"That still does not…explain why you are…here."

"I am prepared to do that," the *Duc* said, "but first, I want to ask you a question."

"What…is it?"

"I want you to look a me, Canéda, while I ask it."

It flashed through Canéda's mind that that was what he had asked her to do once before, and because she was afraid of what she would see in his eyes, and more afraid of the strange feeling that was seeping over her, she shook her head.

How could she explain to him that now he was there now he was talking it was as if she was coming back to life?

The stone in her breast was melting away. She could feel strange unexpected thrills running through her almost as if they were the green buds of spring opening in the sunshine.

She could feel him close beside her, feel the strange vibrations of which she had always been conscious, emanating from him, and she wanted, she thought crazily, to turn around, to touch him, to make sure he was real.

"I told you to look at me, Canéda," the *Duc* said.

He had been speaking in English ever since he had come into the room and it seemed to Canéda that he was giving her an order almost in the same way that she ordered Ariel to obey her.

Then she was afraid, not of him, but of her own feelings, afraid that if she looked into his grey eyes she would forget everything else, and he would see how much she loved him.

Frantically, she tried to say to herself: "He is married…he is married," but somehow the words meant nothing.

All she could think was that he was there, that she vibrated to his voice, and whatever he asked of her it would be impossible to refuse.

"Look at me, Canéda."

Now the words were not a command, but a plea, so entreating that it was utterly impossible to do anything but obey.

Slowly, because she was trembling, Canéda turned around.

She faced him, but she did not raise her eyes. Instead they were on his well-tied, white starched stock.

The *Duc* did not speak, he did not move, he only waited until as if it was impossible to resist him any longer, Canéda raised her eyes to his.

Then as she expected, as they looked at each other she thought, that everything else was meaningless, except the knowledge that he was there, and she belonged to him.

The *Duc* looked at her for what seemed a very long moment. Then he said slowly, as if he was choosing his words with care:

"Answer me truthfully, Canéda, what did you feel when I kissed you in the Château, and I thought, but I could not believe it to be true, that I was the first man ever to touch your lips?"

"The...only man," Canéda whispered and her voice was hardly audible.

She saw a light come into the *Duc's* eyes, and he said:

"Your first kiss, *le premier fois,* and what did it mean to you?"

"I...I do not think I can...tell you."

"Tell me!"

Again it was a command and because she felt shy, Canéda wished to take her eyes from his, and yet it was impossible.

He held her captive, and although he was not even touching her, it was impossible to escape.

153

"Tell me!" he insisted.

"There are...no words to describe it...you carried me into the sky...and we were no longer...human...but part of the moon...the stars and the sun...and...and...God."

Her voice trembled on the last word, and now the *Duc* reached out his arms and pulled her against him roughly.

"And after that," he asked, "did you think I could lose you? That is exactly how I felt, my darling, and you are mine!"

As he said the last words his lips were on hers and at the touch of them Canéda felt as if the Heavens opened and lifted her out of the misery and depression she had felt ever since she had left Saumac, into the light that had seemed to envelop her once before when the *Duc* had kissed her.

His lips were demanding and fiercely insistent, as if he forced her to acknowledge his supremacy and his ownership of her.

At the same time she felt that he was wooing her and she surrendered herself to the wonder of his kiss as if he was the victor so that she could no longer fight against him.

Only when he raised his head did she say incoherently because the words were forced from her:

"I...I...love...you!"

"Say it again," the *Duc* said. "Say it so that I need not be mistaken in knowing that you are really saying it."

"I love you...I love...you!" Canéda cried, and because it was so overwhelming, she hid her face against his neck.

He held her very close before he said:

"I have been so afraid, so desperately afraid that I was mistaken, and yet, how could what we both felt that night by anything but real?"

"It was...very real to...me," Canéda murmured.

The *Duc* put his hand under her chin and turned her face up to his.

She thought he would kiss her, but instead he looked

down at her, and she thought there was a different expression on his face, softer and more gentle than before.

She knew too that there was an expression of love in his eyes that she had always wanted to see.

"You are so beautiful!" he said. "So absurdly and ridiculously beautiful! How could you crucify me as you did by running away in that wicked way?"

"I...I was...frightened."

"I am not surprised! How could you do anything so outrageous, so disgraceful as to get yourself into such a position?"

Canéda felt the blood rising in her cheeks at his words, and yet when she would have hidden her face again, he prevented her from doing so.

"I am very, very angry with you," he said, but there was no anger in the tone of his voice.

"You swear...you did not...tell...Harry?" she asked.

"No. But I will make sure, as I know he would want me to, that you will never do anything like that again."

"And you have...forgiven me?"

"If I made you as unhappy as I was myself," the *Duc* said, "then I suppose we are what you would call 'quits'."

"I was very...very unhappy when you would not...look at me...or speak to...me."

"I was afraid you might not care."

Canéda knew that in fact she had felt despairingly there was nothing left in life because she had lost him.

Then once again she remembered, almost as if it loomed over her like a great menacing cloud, that he was married.

"I am sure it is very wrong of...us to talk like...this."

"Wrong?" he questioned.

She felt for the words in which to express the truth. Then he said as if again he had read her thoughts:

"Suppose now you ask my why I have come to see your brother?"

"I cannot...imagine why you...should do so," Canéda said, "unless you wished to see his...horses."

It struck her that must be the explanation.

There was a smile on the *Duc's* lips as he replied:

"I am certainly impressed by them, but I am deeply concerned with something far more important – his sister."

"Y...you told Harry...that?" Canéda asked incredulously.

"Because I wished to behave conventionally in England at any rate, I told your brother that I hoped to marry you."

"To...to marry me?"

Canéda was so astonished that she moved away from his encircling arms to stand staring at him wide-eyed.

"B...but I was told...I understood..."

"That I had a wife. That was true until three years ago."

"She is dead?"

"She died," the *Duc* said quietly.

"But...no...one knew..."

"Why should they?" he asked. "I have never discussed my private affairs with anyone, not even my relatives. Ever since I was first married I have been embittered by what I suffered, and I consider it my business, and my business alone."

He spoke sharply. Then he said in a different tone of voice:

"I had decided never to marry again. I thought myself completely self-sufficient with my horses and Saumac until – I met you."

"Is that...true?" Canéda asked.

"I think you know it is true without my saying any more," the *Duc* said.

"I wanted you to love me," Canéda said. "I do not wish you to feel now that because I am who I am you are being pressured into marriage. After all...you asked me something...very different."

156

"That was entirely your fault," the *Duc* replied, "but I knew when I kissed you that I would never let you go, and that to make sure you did not leave me, I must make you my wife."

"Did you...really feel...that?"

"I swear it," the *Duc* answered. "But that still does not make me any less shocked at the risks you ran in behaving as you did."

Canéda smiled.

Because of what he had told her, because he had said that he loved her and asked her to marry him, she felt as if there was music playing all around her and the air was sparkling with light.

"It may have been outrageous...and you may have been...shocked," she said, "but if I had not let you...kiss me that night...on the moon, you might never have known how much...we loved each other or that it was...impossible to forget."

"You are twisting yourself out of a very difficult situation," the *Duc* said accusingly.

But as he spoke he moved towards Canéda and put his arms around her.

"How soon are you goung to marry me?" he asked, "I do not intend to wait long."

"I have not yet accepted your proposal," she replied provacatively.

"Arc you trying to refuse me?" he asked.

As he spoke his lips moved over the softness of her cheek. Then they outlined the top of her mouth, then her small pointed chin.

It gave her a strange feeling. Then as she longed for him to kiss her, her lips ready and yearning for his, he sought the softness of her neck.

He felt the quiver that ran through her as strange sensations made her feel wildly excited yet weak and submissive.

Then as her breath came quickly from between her lips

he kissed her and once again they were in the light coming from the Heavens and it was impossible to think of anything else but that she was his, and they were one person in mind, heart and soul.

Only as Canéda felt as if the wonder of it was almost too great to be borne did the *Duc* say in a voice that he tried to keep steady:

"Now tell me when you will marry me."

"Now! This…moment!"

He laughed, and it was a sound of triumph.

"That is what I wanted you to say, my precious one."

He held her close once again, as if enfolding her protectively against the world, and against anything which might hurt her.

"I love you! I adore you! I worship you!" he said. "Will you be happy with me on my corner of the moon?"

"I would be happy with you…anywhere…anywhere in the…world," Canéda replied, "but especially happy on your…moon as long as we can be…together."

"You may be sure of that," the *Duc* answered, "and I am not returning to France without you, just in case you are, as you told me when we first met, a shooting-star, whom it is impossible to capture."

He kissed her forehead as he spoke. Then he said:

"On your first visit to France you not only found me, but discovered your mother's family, whom you love even though your brother tells me you went there prepared to hate them."

"I love them and feel so…sorry for…them."

"Before I came to England," the *Duc* said, "I talked to the Manager of your grandfather's estate and with the other landlords in the district. We evolved a plan for the future which will not make the loss of the vines quite so bad as it appears at the moment."

"I am so, so glad!" Canéda cried. "What can they do?"

"It is a question of a different sort of farming," the *Duc* explained. "The land is good, and I think they could produce a continuous succession of crops, rather different from those in other regions. Tobacco is one, strawberries another, besides accelerating the sales of what is a particular luxury in France – truffles."

Canéda gave a little cry of joy.

"If the de Bantôme estate can do all that, then they will not be so hard up and will not feel so desperate over the loss of their vines."

"It will mean a lot of hard work, and imagination," the *Duc* said, "but your Uncle René, who you have not met, is prepared to make every effort, and so I think will Armand, when he settles down."

Canéda gave a little sigh.

"You are so clever," she said, "and with you to help them I know they will be all right."

"We will help them together," the *Duc* said, "just as, my precious little love, we will do everything together, you and I, especially schooling our horses."

"I thought I was barred from the Riding-School," Canéda teased.

"You will certainly not be allowed there when the young officers are having their lessons," the *Duc* said. "Not only would you make it impossible for them to concentrate on what I am telling them, but I shall be an extremely jealous husband."

His voice deepened as he said:

"If I see you looking in that provocative way from under your eye-lashes at any other man, I shall most certainly lock you up in the dungeons, and you will never, my adorable one, never again wear a pink riding-habit."

Canéda laughed.

"I wanted to attract your attention."

"You did that, but I will not allow any other man to notice you in the same way."

Canéda looked at him with a little smile on her lips. Then he said:

"Of course I am mad to give up my quiet, well-organised life for you! I am well aware of the tortures you will inflict on me!"

"You do not...*have* to...marry me."

"You are not suggesting any other relationship, I hope?"

Canéda blushed and said quickly:

"No, of course not! I was only saying that if you wish to be free you can go...back to Saumac and...leave me...here."

"And if I did, what would you feel?"

As if the *Duc* frightened her, Canéda held onto him.

"I could not bear to be so unhappy again. I love you...I love you! Please, do not...leave me!"

"I will never do that," the *Duc* replied. "You are mine, now and for ever, and my naughty one, whether you like it or not, the moon will be a prison from which you will never escape."

"I will never want to," Canéda tried to say, but his lips were on hers, and she only knew that once she was in the moon and in the *Duc's* arms all her dreams would come true.